Dear Reader,

Balmy breezes, sa... waters as far as th... irresistible, physic... people time and a... other off-the-beaten-track lands? Or is it the discovery of a lifestyle that seems to progress at a different pace? And what is it in a person that seeks those things—a particular personality trait or event in their life? For me, it was wondering about these things that provided the "what if" kernel that grew into an island called Turnabout and the people whose lives are forever changed by their experiences there.

I don't know why I'm always surprised at the way the inhabitants of my stories become such a part of my life as I write. Yet they do. I laugh their laughter, cry their tears and triumph in their happily-ever-after. Mel and Luke were no different. I hope you'll enjoy their tale, and maybe—during the time it takes to turn these pages, at least—you'll share some of the magic of Turnabout.

Peace,

Allison

One More Chance
ALLISON LEIGH

SILHOUETTE®

SPECIAL EDITION™

*First published in Great Britain 2006
Silhouette Books, Eton House, 18-24 Paradise Road,
Richmond, Surrey TW9 1SR*

© Allison Lee Davidson 2003

*ISBN-13: 978 0 373 60472 2
ISBN-10:0 373 60472 6*

23-1006

*Printed and bound in Spain
by Litografia Rosés S.A., Barcelona*

ALLISON LEIGH

There is a saying that you can never be too rich or too thin. Allison doesn't believe that, but she does believe that you can never have enough bookshelves or enough books! When her stories find a way into the hearts—and onto the bookshelves—of others, Allison says she feels she's done something right. Making her home in Arizona with her family, she enjoys hearing from her readers at: Allison@ allisonleigh.com or PO Box 40772, Mesa, AZ 85274-0772, USA.

To Dar, Susan, Linda and Deb.

Here's to many more pages, more laughs, more learning and more successes.

Love, A

Chapter 1

She was crying.

Despite the low rush of the soft waves foaming up over the white sand, and despite the way she'd pressed her head against her drawn-up knees, Luke could hear her quiet sobs.

Not even sobs.

The woman was weeping.

He didn't really know why he considered there to be a difference. But there was. He'd seen it time and again in his line of work. Nervous tears. Choking sobs of despair. Weak sobs of disbelieving relief.

He recognized the difference, and the woman sitting on the sand, not even far enough up the beach to keep the folds of her ghostly pale dress from being soaked by the froth of water that advanced and retreated over her feet, was definitely weeping.

Luke's boots slowed, dragged to a stop in the sand

and he shoved his hands into his pockets, turning his gaze from the huddled woman to the moon-gilded ocean.

Turnabout was the name of the island on which he stood. Doing a turnabout was pretty much what he wanted to do. A turnabout off this dinky island situated well off the coast of San Diego, and make tracks straight back to Phoenix. Even though his work there wasn't exactly a walk through the park these days, either, he could have climbed underneath the hood of the old Camaro he was restoring and used the smell of grease and the heft of heavy tools to forget the way he'd failed with a far more delicate task.

He blew out an impatient breath, glancing again at the woman.

She hadn't budged.

Which left him with few choices.

He hadn't really wanted to come to Turnabout in the first place. Hadn't wanted to do anything but keep going over the whole thing, endlessly trying to figure what he'd done wrong, wallowing in the guilt of it. But now he was here and the only thing he really wanted was a clean bed under him. In order to get that clean bed, he had to get the key to the cottage, and the key was with Maisy Fielding, the proprietress of the inn, who—according to the hand-lettered sign that had been taped to the door of the deserted inn—could be found at the community center. ''The big building,'' the sign had further elaborated. ''Straight up the road.''

So what had Luke done? Headed straight up the road? Hell no.

He'd felt the call of the beach and, dumping his duffel bag on the inn porch, he'd walked, not up the road to the big building, but in the opposite direction.

He'd listened to enough of his boss's infernal stories about this place to know that there was only one town on Turnabout, with one main road crossing the length of the island. It didn't matter where you were, Jason Frame had said time and again, if you walked along the beach, sooner or later you'd end up at one or the other end of that road, which led to the town.

Luke glanced again at the woman. She wasn't curled in a ball anymore, but had propped her elbows on her bent knees. Her hands covered her face and her hair streamed back from her head on the breeze, looking like ribbons of silver in the moonlight.

Dammit.

He should have taken the short route and stuck to the road, because his choices now were limited to turning around and going back toward the inn or continuing on past the weeping woman.

The beach was a graceful curve of thick, fine sand, but it was increasingly narrow toward her and there was no way on God's windy shore that he could pass by her without disturbing her solitude. Walking all the way back to the inn to start over again held zero appeal. Walking all the way back to the inn to just wait until Maisy Fielding returned was even lower on the scale. According to the sign, the party at the "big building" that she was attending would probably last until dawn.

If Luke hadn't heard at least a dozen of Jason's stories, he'd have written off that particular nugget of information as pure exaggeration.

He started forward, staying close to the cliff wall and

keeping his eyes straight ahead. Away from the hunched figure that sat on the wet sand, letting the edge of water flow up and over her.

Why didn't she move out of the water, at least?

Keep going, Luke.

He was almost even with her, now. She hadn't made a single movement betraying her awareness of him, yet she had to know he was there. Was the woman nuts? Completely unaware of her own safety? For all she knew he could be some scumbag, intent on harm.

Yet she just sat there. Getting soaked in the water.

Weeping.

He couldn't do it. He wanted to. He tried to. But he couldn't do it. He couldn't just walk past the woman as if she weren't there.

He exhaled a long breath and veered toward her, shrugging out of his jacket.

"You must be cold," he said quietly as he approached her from the side, not particularly interested in scaring the tar out of her. He didn't want her mistaking him for some scumbag.

Her shoulders jerked a little, but she didn't look at him. That was okay. He didn't intend to hang around long.

"Here." His fingers grazed her shoulders as he leaned over to drape his jacket around her, confirming the obvious. She *was* cold. It was the middle of January and she was wearing a white dress that didn't even cover her arms. "You should move back out of the water before you get even more wet."

She slowly tilted her head, the ripples of long, pale

hair hiding her profile from him. She started to hand back his jacket.

"Keep it."

She hesitated and he took the matter out of her hands by simply dropping it once more around her shoulders.

Her slender fingers slowly closed around the lapels. She pulled them close. The jacket easily eclipsed her slender torso. The bottom of it folded over against the wet sand.

"You're very kind." Her voice was faint, husky.

He almost laughed. Most people would never associate him with that particular trait. He was good at what he did—at least he had been. But kind?

Not lately.

He shoved his hands into the pockets of his jeans and peered down the coastline. "Are you just visiting Turnabout?"

She silently shook her head.

"Then you'd know the community center. Is it far?"

She didn't answer immediately. When she did, it was hardly illuminating. "Not terribly," she said.

He looked at her down-turned head. The moonlight, what there was of it between the clouds striping the night sky, made her hair look white and he wondered, briefly, what color it would be in sunlight.

His boots were being baptized by salt water, same as the bottom of his jacket. His jaw felt tight. "You really should move back on the beach. You're getting soaked."

He heard her faint sigh. "I'm already soaked." But she rose to her feet and he automatically caught her arms when she swayed. She was taller than he'd expected.

The wind caught her long hair, blowing it across her face, blowing it against his arms, his chest. Her hair was silky. Soft. And something inside him warmed.

He brushed the strands away even as she caught at it with both hands, trying to tame it back.

His jacket started to slide from her shoulders and he caught it before it fell away completely. Hell, he grabbed it before the thing landed in the water that was currently ruining his boots. It helped a little with her long hair, when he pulled it back up on her shoulders, capturing some of the length beneath the collar before the wind could snatch at it again.

She didn't make a sound, but the waves of tension rolling off her were every bit as real as the ones pushing against the shore.

He didn't have time for this—to be waylaid by some female who had desperation seeping from her pores. All he wanted was the damn key to his damn cottage. All he wanted was a clean bed, a decent night of sleep.

All he wanted was some peace.

So he'd keep walking and find that "big building." Right.

He still hadn't seen her face. "Are you all right?"

"Please go. Here." She started to remove the jacket.

Annoyance rose swiftly inside him. Too swift.

Yeah. He needed peace.

He bracketed her hands with his, keeping the jacket in place. Her wrists were so slender, her hands so narrow, his hand easily encompassed both. "You're shivering." *Get going, Luke.* "I told you to keep it."

She said something, but the wind whipped her soft words into oblivion. Being able to hear her certainly wasn't helped by the way she kept her head lowered, her chin ducked. He bent his head closer. "What?"

"I said—" she finally lifted her head "—I can't." This time, her low voice was clear. He still barely heard.

The face she'd lifted was beautiful. The pain etched in it, though, was what stopped him cold.

He was acutely grateful for the less-than-brilliant moonlight, for the shadows. He wasn't sure he could stand to see this woman's sheer torment by the cold light of day.

He wasn't proud of it, but he still acknowledged the truth of it.

"It's just a jacket," he murmured. "I have others."

Her fingertips shifted, a small movement that he nevertheless noted. She was testing the feel of the leather with those narrow hands.

"I'm not the one shivering," he added quietly.

At that, her trembling increased. It was visible the way she shuddered and quaked. She drew her brows together. "I c-can't seem to s-stop."

"Your feet are bare and you're half-soaked." So why did he know that the shivers racking her body had little to do with external conditions and a lot more to do with whatever weight was crushing her heart? "Let me walk you home."

"That's not n-necessary."

His hand rasped over his jaw and he sighed, finally acknowledging another truth inside him. "I can't walk away from you like this."

She shook her hair out of her face, but it simply blew back across it. "Why not? You're a stranger to m-me."

He didn't even bother to answer that. "Do you have shoes somewhere?"

She was peering at him. "Why are you here?"

"Shoes?"

Her brows drew together again. "I don't know. I think they may have gone out on the tide."

He sighed. Then he put his arms around her and simply picked her up, right out of the water.

She went stiff as a board.

His hair was too long and he badly needed a shave, so he had no cause for offense. "If I were going to hurt you, I could have already done it," he said flatly, and carried her out of reach of the water. Then he set her down.

She shivered, but he could see some stiffening of her spine in the way her posture straightened and her head went back. "I'm not afraid of you."

"Well, if you had a lick of sense, you would be." The irritation in him came from nowhere. Again, it came too easily.

"You're on an island," she said. "A small one, with only one, tiny little port managed by Diego Montoya. If you want to get on or off the island, you're going to have to deal with him, a fact you surely know as…well—" she gestured "—here you are. Obviously, anyone coming to Turnabout to cause harm would be a fool as there is no place to run."

He ventured a guess that there were other ways a determined person could get around, but kept the thought to himself. He'd arrived by private charter and had not seen hide nor hair of anyone. Maybe Diego's diligence didn't extend to missing a party any more than Maisy's extended to making a key easily available for expected guests. "There you go, then. You're as safe as a babe in her mama's arms." *Get going, Luke.*

She shifted, not responding.

He studied her. She really was one tall drink of water. The top of her head reached his jaw. "Do you want to talk about it?"

"No."

Fair enough. He didn't want to talk about his thoughts, either.

Silence twined between them. He needed to keep moving. Get the key. Get some sleep.

He needed to stop telling himself things like that, when it was obvious he was doing no such thing.

"I'm Luke," he finally said.

She didn't immediately respond. She adjusted her grip on the jacket, pulled it closer around her and cast him a quick glance that struck him as wary and longing all in one.

Maybe his sheer exhaustion had him hallucinating. *Longing?*

She shifted again and finally spoke. "I'm Mel."

A more feminine Mel he'd never before seen. "Well, Mel, you need to get dry before you end up sick."

She looked out over the water, her profile pure. "I've never been sick a day in my life," she said quietly. There was a wealth of sadness in her voice.

A tall drink of water, yeah. But more like a narrow crystal glass that would shatter if gripped too tightly. "Then you're luckier than most."

Her head slowly turned and she looked up at him, her eyes dark and unreadable. "Am I?"

He couldn't help himself. He brushed his thumb over her soft lips, tracing the frown that had drawn down the corners. Something dark and beckoning that had filled the air when he wasn't paying attention tugged at him again. "Lucky to have good health? Yeah. Don't wish away something that most people would consider a blessing."

He could feel those unreadable eyes studying him. Searching. "Why are you here?"

It was the second time she had asked and there was no point in pretending he thought she referred to his reasons for being on the island. "I don't know," he said. "To lend you my jacket, maybe."

"Please don't be kind," she whispered. "I don't think I can take it. Not…not tonight."

He exhaled a rough breath. "I'm not kind," he said flatly. Then he put his hands on her shoulders, which were buried under his pricey leather jacket, and gently pulled her against his chest.

He felt a sob work through her. Then another.

How many women had he held while they cried? Too many to count. None of them had ever made his throat tighten. None had made his head ache, deep, behind his eyes.

Then he felt her hands on his chest. Her fingers curling into his shirt. She was shaking like a leaf and, God, in that moment he wanted nothing more than to take away her pain, give her some peace, some respite from whatever plagued her soul.

Luke. The healer.

What a damned bloody joke.

His arms went around her back, one hand cupping the back of her silky head. He could feel the warmth of her tears against his neck, the desperation in her hands and the strength of her arms as they circled his waist.

His jaw ached and he swallowed. Hard.

"I don't want to hurt anymore." Her voice was broken, nearly inaudible against him.

Neither did he.

He held her closer. "It's okay."

Was he speaking to her, or to himself?

Did it even matter? He didn't know that anything would ever be okay again.

He closed his eyes, closed off the unbearable thought. But it kept sneaking back in, and he pressed his cheek to the top of her hair, inhaling the scent of the sea, the sand and her. It helped keep the yawning abyss at bay.

So he held her like that a while longer.

She thought he was kind.

Truth was, he was only being selfish.

He finally lifted his head and stared out at the dark water behind her. The clouds had covered the moon again. The wind was getting stronger. If it weren't for the warmth of her body pressed against him, he'd be cold, too.

He *was* cold, as he gently nudged a few inches of space between them. "Let me get you home."

"There's no one there." She spoke evenly, with no tears thickening her voice, no sobs breaking. The statement was all the more bereft because of it.

Though they were no longer standing in the water, he felt suddenly as if he were drowning in depths he should have been smart enough to avoid. Because she was warm against him, and very, very female. The face she turned up to him was vulnerable, and all he'd have to do would be tilt his head a few inches and his mouth would be on hers.

He thought about putting a little more distance between them. Thought about it, and did nothing to accomplish it. "Mel." Then he didn't know what to say.

Her hands slid up his back. Came around and glided up to his neck. Only his arms around her kept his jacket from falling away from her.

"Who is waiting at home for you, Luke?" Her words whispered over his jaw. "Who've you come to Turnabout to visit?"

He had no family left, anymore. And he'd just gotten rid of the last connection to the one piece of family who'd mattered. He realized he'd wrapped his fingers in her hair. "There's no one waiting for me."

She closed her eyes, pressed her temple briefly to his chin. "I'm sorry."

The throbbing was back again inside his head. "Why?"

She shook her head a little. "Maybe for the same reason you stopped to put your jacket around a stranger."

"Mel."

He saw her throat work. "Do you..." She stopped and moistened her lips. "Do you ever wonder if you'll make it through to morning, Luke?"

He couldn't take it. He ran his thumb down the trail

left by her tears. Her cheek was cool, velvet over finely arched bones. He was barely aware that her hair was blowing around them again, like a curtain of silk.

Her lips parted softly and her lashes fell. She turned her cheek into his hand. ''Warm.'' The word was more a sigh, and good sense, caution, and any claim to wisdom that he might have possessed scattered like dust thrown in the wind.

He tugged her head back and knew that it went willingly.

He lowered his mouth over hers, the briefest of tastes. And knew that her lips clung to his, silently asking for more.

When he lifted his head instead, searching her eyes for…what? Permission? Hesitation? All he saw was the same thing tightening his throat, exploding in his veins.

All he saw was need.

Chapter 2

Luke gathered her closer. Felt the quick breath she drew and the tightening of her fingers around his neck, in his hair.

He sucked in a sharp breath, his forehead touching hers. "Tell me to stop."

"Stop." She twisted her head around, pressing a quick kiss to his lips. "Stop." The tip of her tongue glided along his lower lip. "Stop."

Right. He stopped her tormenting little nibbles by kissing her. Flat out. His hands cradled her head, tilting it to suit him. Her lips parted and he tasted the low moan she gave as her tongue dueled, then danced, with his.

Heat blasted inside him, not at all cooled by the night wind. Sanity reared and he jerked back his head, stepping away, letting go of her. The cliff wall behind him stopped him short.

The jacket he'd worked so hard to keep around her slid off her shoulders. Her hands clasped together and she covered her mouth with them.

The gauzy white fabric of her damp dress blew around her legs, reaching toward him, fluttering over his jeans. Her hands slowly fell to her sides. "I'm sorry," she said, her voice raw. "I'm so sorry."

He needed to get out of there. Before he did something really stupid. "Mel—"

She shook her head. "I can't believe I threw myself at you like that, not when you're just being k—"

"Don't say it."

"—kind."

They stared at each other.

She moved first, reaching down to pick up the jacket that had fallen to the sand. She shook it a little and carefully smoothed her hand over it, brushing away the grains that stuck to it. "Here." She held it out to him. "The, um, the community center is about a mile up the beach, still. If you watch for it, you'll see a set of narrow steps in the cliff. They'll lead you right up to the building. You can't miss it. It's the biggest building on the island. And, um, well, everyone in town is there tonight."

"Except you."

Her hair was blowing madly, hiding her face again. "I was there. Earlier. I, uh, I didn't stay." She made a faint sound. "Obviously."

"I didn't kiss you out of kindness."

Her hand with the jacket dropped a little. "Oh." She stiffened her arm once more. "Well. Here."

He reached out, but closed his hand over hers instead

of the jacket. His thumb traced her tightly clenched knuckles. "Yes. Sometimes I wonder if I'll make it to morning." He finally answered the question he'd avoided. "Kissing you wasn't being kind."

"Okay."

She made to pull her hand back from him and he knew she didn't believe what he'd said. He held on. "How old are you?" A damn sight younger than his own forty-one, he knew for a fact. The moonlight wasn't *that* faint.

"Old enough to know better," she said on a sigh. "I'm sorry."

"Dammit, stop apologizing. If you won't let me get you home, then at least go with me up to the community center. You said everyone in town is there."

She shook her head. "No."

"Did you have an argument with someone there? Your boyfriend? Is that why you're upset?"

She tugged her hair away from her face, holding it in a loose ponytail with her hand. "No. There's no boyfriend. There's nobody. Look, I'm so—" He saw the long, lovely line of her throat work. "You should go now. It's probably going to rain soon. You'll get wet if you linger."

"What about you?"

"I'm used to it."

Which made him wonder how many nights she sat, alone on the beach, while she let the rain come down on her.

"I haven't sat in the rain since I was a kid." He hadn't enjoyed it then, mostly because it meant his mother had gone off and forgotten to leave a door open for him and his sister.

Her teeth caught her soft lip for a moment. "Stay out here much longer and you'll undoubtedly get a reminder of it," she said. "But I'm afraid it would probably ruin your jacket."

He didn't give a damn about the jacket. Staying on the beach—with her—held a much higher cost. "I want to kiss you again."

Her fist went slack, the jacket falling unheeded, and he turned her hand in his, pressing his palm to hers. It was oddly intimate, he realized, feeling her slender palm flush against his larger one. He heard her inhale sharply and wondered if it was because of his admission, or because of their hands.

"But I don't want to stop at a kiss," he continued evenly. "And I don't take what's not offered, so say the wo—"

"Then don't stop." Tension vibrated off her.

Heat collected at the base of his spine. *What the hell were they doing here?* "Mel."

She stepped forward, over the jacket that now lay in a heap on the sand, and pressed their joined hands over her heart. "Do you feel that?"

He felt her heartbeat charging against his palm. He felt the soft weight of her breast against his fingers.

"My heart," she said, her tone more than a little ragged, "stopped hurting when you kissed me. I don't want you to stop. I don't care what you think of me, what it makes me. I just want—" she shook her head sharply, pressing her lips together "—to get through tonight. I want the pain to stop for just…one…night."

Then her gaze met his. "Isn't that what you're looking for, too?"

He started to deny it. But what good would it do? She could have been describing him as easily as she described herself.

One night. Two strangers.

"I didn't come out here looking for an easy—"

"I know," she cut him off. "I know. Nor did I. Despite the way it probably appeared."

"I don't think that, Mel." He didn't. It hadn't even occurred to him. He'd had plenty of experience with women who had thrown themselves at him. He could recognize the difference.

She pressed her lips together for a moment. Her gaze dropped to their hands. She slowly slipped her fingers between his, curling them down. He curled his fingers, too, and she seemed to sigh a little as their hands linked even more firmly.

"I came out here looking for peace," she said softly. "Just…some peace." Her fingers tightened a little. "It wasn't working. The beach. The moonlight. It's always worked before. But not tonight." She moistened her lips and looked at him, and he felt the punch of it. It felt as if she were looking down inside him.

With recognition.

He searched her wide-eyed gaze for a long while.

Then he tugged on her hand.

She came willingly.

The wind blew, and he turned his back to it, until he could protect her from the worst of it. He ran his hands down her back, slowly tracing the length of her spine. He thought about the rough, rocky wall behind her. The fact that he hadn't shaved in days, and the fact that her skin was soft. Tender.

"We should get in out of the cold."

Her mouth searched out his. "Now." Her lips moved against his. "I don't want to wait. I know if we have to walk you'll change your mind."

"You know that, do you? Know me so well?"

He felt her lips curve in the faintest of smiles. "Do you really want a mile-long walk, Luke?"

He liked hearing his name on her lips. He liked her lips, period.

Her fingers scrabbled at the sides of his shirt, tugging the tails loose. He sucked in a harsh breath when those fingers slid over his abdomen, slipping just inside the waist of his jeans. He caught her hand in his, halting the movement before she could go any further. "Maybe not," he allowed.

She made a soft sound, somewhere between a moan and a sob, and he swallowed it with his mouth, letting her hands go where they wanted.

His fingers, ordinarily known for their deftness, felt clumsy and thick as he worked a half-dozen buttons free. She was bare beneath the lightweight fabric.

Bare and warm and impossibly soft. Her head fell back as he kissed her jaw, her heart skittered when he slid his palm over her. She whispered his name, or maybe it was just wishful thinking on his part, when he tasted the long column of her throat, dawdled over her clavicle then slid down the valley between her breasts. She arched, making that low humming sound in her throat again, when he dragged his thumbs over her nipples, feeling them draw up even more tightly.

Her hands abandoned his strained fly and sank into his hair when he caught one crest between his lips. She tasted sweet, as warm and heady as the summer day on which she ought to have been wearing the fragile white dress. Then she twisted, pushing the thin straps of the dress from her shoulders, and he was vaguely aware of the fabric falling away from her slender torso, halting at her waist, her hips, where it fitted snug against her taut body.

He tore at the buttons of his shirt, then pulled her up, flush against him. Skin against skin. Curve against angle and felt satisfaction roar inside him at the contact.

Satisfaction that wasn't nearly satisfying enough.

He felt her knees go, and easily took her weight, glad to take it, because it brought her that much closer against him. Because his senses were consumed by her, because finally there was no room for thoughts, for regrets, for guilt.

There was only Mel.

Mel, who'd twined her long legs around his hips. Mel, whose breath was as unsteady as his. Mel, who was prying open his button fly with neither elegance nor finesse. But he didn't care, because she managed to get the job done even as his fingers traced the path of the thin strip of soft fabric that stretched over her hip and found her beneath, even softer, even warmer.

She shuddered against him, humming, moaning his name, and somehow they ended up on the sand. The folds of her skirt fell over him as he pulled off her panties and she sank down on him, taking him in, bowing over him, all soft summer-sweet flesh and silken arms, rushing around him as surely as the surf rushed the sand.

Colors exploded in his head, fire exploded inside him. But he struggled for restraint, because, dammit, there was a piece of his brain still firing on more than half a cylinder and he knew there was something dangerous in this insanity. His hands tightened around her hips. Hips that were smooth and taut and unbelievably soft all at once. Hips that moved against his in a dance as old as time but just then felt as new as dawn. ''Mel—''

Her lips covered his, her body tightening, beckoning.

He rolled over and caught her hands with one of his because her touch was going to be the death of him, and he hadn't had nearly enough.

She was shuddering wildly, and he heard a groan, vaguely aware it came from him, as he thrust deeper, wanting more, wanting to imprint himself on her the way she had on him. Wanting to hear the gasp in her voice as she cried his name, and feel every ripple work through her flesh that gloved him.

Then she cried out, and Luke felt her quake, deep inside where he couldn't tell where he ended and she began. Shocking pleasure ripped through him, splintered his gut, rocketed from the base of his skull to the depths of his soul.

And without another single coherent thought, he came, pouring hot and hard and fast, into Mel.

Chapter 3

Later, silent, Mel walked with him to the community center. The wind had died down until it was practically nonexistent. Without the wind, and with the clouds pressing down on the night, the temperature seemed to have actually risen. Still she wore his jacket.

She pointed out the steep stairs that had been carved by some ambitious soul into the cliff wall and tried to tell him that he ought to go first, as he wasn't familiar with the steps.

He just looked at her and, with a small sound in her throat, she climbed up before him, holding her long skirt gathered to one side of her thighs.

He shook his head as he wrapped his hand over the iron rail and began the ascent. His intention had been a simple matter of safety. If she fell on the dark, steep steps, he could catch her.

He looked up at her making her way.

Whatever his reasons, it was a helluva view.

It was also a helluva climb. And, by the time they made it to the top, the clouds had finally made good on their threat as it began to rain. A soft misting of water that was nothing at all like the sometimes vicious, generally brief, rainstorms he was used to in Phoenix.

Mel looked back down at him, and he could see the faint smile on her lips. "I warned you." Then she was climbing again. The flimsy sandals of hers that they'd finally found on the beach tangled in a hank of seaweed, made little squishing sounds with each step she took.

Maybe what they'd done out there on the beach had been as foolish as anything he'd ever done, but he'd be hanged if he could regret it.

Not when he thought about the way she'd giggled. Afterward.

He'd still been wearing his boots. They'd had sand everywhere.

She'd giggled.

And he'd laughed.

Then she'd pressed her soft lips to his, and they'd done it all, again.

Even now, he could feel the faint tug at his lips. He'd be lucky if he wasn't grinning like some damn fool teenager who'd just discovered that paradise wasn't a pretty Pacific island, but a warm place in one particular woman's arms.

He'd wanted some peace.

Well, he felt as peaceful now as he had in years.

Maybe ever. There was also no more sign of Mel's tears.

He joined her at the top of the steps and frowned when she sidestepped the hand he held out. But maybe it was his imagination, because she'd turned and was pointing. "There's the community center."

Luke looked, nowhere near as interested in the place as he had been earlier. But even his humor was pricked at what he saw. The biggest building on the island wasn't really all that large. It was single storied, multi-windowed and shot off in wings from a central section in an assortment of directions. But the sign over the door that proclaimed it The Biggest Building On Turnabout was bold and unmistakable.

"People on Turnabout have a sense of humor," he said.

"A bit," she allowed blandly. She walked across the parking area—a wide pad of gravel, short-cropped grass, and an occasional patch of smooth cement that was covered with dozens of bicycles, a few Radio Flyers, and only three actual automobiles.

"There aren't very many cars on Turnabout," she told him, noting the focus of his attention.

He had to concentrate on not staring at her. In the moonlight she'd been beautiful. The closer they drew to the brightly lit community center, the more he realized just how exquisite her face really was. He scrambled for the thread of conversation.

So much for his supposed brilliance.

Cars. That was it. Not many cars on the island. "Too expensive to have them shipped here?"

She didn't seem to have noticed his conversational

lapse. "That. But mostly because there isn't much that isn't just as easily reached by foot or bicycle."

"There's a road." He could see it. A thin ribbon of tarmac, admittedly, but still a road.

"Yes, but it's the only road and the Turns are perfectly happy with it that way."

"Turns?"

"The islanders who've been born and raised here call themselves Turns. You know. As in Turn—"

"—about." Luke stepped around a two-seater bicycle. "Yeah. I get it. So, do you call yourself a Turn, too?"

She smiled faintly, glancing very briefly up at him. "There is only one person on Turnabout who wasn't born here who is considered a Turn."

"Who's that?" He was more interested in knowing where *she* was from, though.

"Maisy Fielding."

The woman who had the key to his cottage.

Luke caught Mel's sidelong glance as they neared the entrance of the community center—two double doors that were propped wide-open despite the late hour and the misting rain. Music and laughter spilled from inside. "What?"

Her hand moved in a low, dismissive wave and the sleeve that she'd pushed up above her wrist slid down over her fingers. "It's nothing," she dismissed. "None of my business."

He closed his hand over her elbow. It felt delicate beneath the leather. "Even after what just happened?"

She flushed. At least, he was fairly sure she flushed. It was hard to tell, given the number of colored lights

strung around the exterior of the building. There were
so many it was like some Christmas elf had run amok.
They were all lit, blinking on and off in a crazed
rhythm of blue, green, red and white.

Jason's wife, who could barely contain herself from
decorating every inch of the clinic before December
even began, would have loved it. Luke had little appreciation for Lydia's efforts, though. To him, Christmas—all holidays really—were just another day of the
week. It wasn't as if those needing care at Sunquest
took the day off every time a holiday rolled around.

Mel still hadn't answered. She brushed her hand over
her hair, swiping at the damp tendrils clinging to her
cheek, managing to look shy and sexy at the same time.
It was a look that probably had every man who met
her wanting to protect her as much as touch her.

She moistened her lips. "Luke, about…that." She
dashed at her hair again. "I don't, um—"

"Don't?" He drew out the word and lifted an eyebrow. "Don't what? Spit it out, Mel, whatever it is."
He already knew he wasn't going to like it.

"Don't think we should, well—"

"Talk about it? Refer to it? Remember it?" He eyed
her. *"Repeat it?"*

She paled. Feeling like an ass, not liking it one bit,
he let go of her arm, stepping back.

"You never said who it is you're visiting here." Her
voice was careful. She'd folded her arms protectively
across her chest.

"I'm not. I told you there was no one waiting for
me."

"At least there's that," she said softly.

"Do you really think I'd have touched you if there were someone else in my life?"

Her lips pressed together for a moment. "I don't really know you well enough to say."

He put his hand under her chin, lifting it. "You say that to me? *Now?*"

Her lashes finally lifted, and he saw her eyes in the light. They were brown. Such a dark brown that he could barely distinguish the pupil from the iris. Her lashes were dark, too. All in all, she was mesmerizing. He'd have thought so, even if he hadn't just made love to her.

She turned her head away from his hand. "I say that because it is true." Her voice was husky. "I, um, I don't even know your last name. If you're on Turnabout for vacation or b-business."

"Business." It was true in a manner of speaking. "And I don't know your last name, either."

She seemed to absorb that. "Summerville," she provided after a moment. "Will you be staying long?"

A part of him recognized the absurdity of their words. This situation. Her panties, torn from her by his hand, were stuffed in his front pocket, and here they were making small talk, near as he could tell. "A week."

"That long."

He laughed shortly, knowing it was only his dark humor rearing its ugly head. "Sorry to disappoint you."

Her cheeks colored again. "I didn't mean it that way."

"Are you certain?"

She didn't answer. Which pretty much *gave* him the answer.

Maybe the sudden hollowness in his stomach was just hunger. And maybe he really was the "kind" man she'd accused him of being.

Right.

Pigs had wings and he was actually entitled to the brief period of peace he'd been afforded.

He shoved his hand through his hair, raking back the too-long strands. "Mel—"

"I just meant that I hoped you had reservations somewhere. For a stay that long, I mean. There aren't that many guest facilities on the island." She spoke fast, her words nearly tumbling over each other.

"I do have reservations. Maisy's Place. That's why I was headed to the community center. There was a sign on the door that said to go there."

She gave a start. "Maisy's? But there was only one reservation for this week. I, um, I help manage the inn and guest cottages for Maisy Fielding," she explained, looking distinctly uncomfortable. "I have for the past few years."

"The reservation was for an associate of mine. Jason Frame. My coming here was a last-minute decision."

Her brows drew together. "You work with Dr. Frame?" Her voice was careful, making Luke wonder at the cause.

He nodded. Started to tell her, but a voice hailed Mel and she whirled around to face the diminutive woman who was hurrying out the double doors.

Short and skinny with a head of corkscrew red curls, the woman stopped, pressing her hand to her chest as she caught her breath. Luke realized she was older than her initial appearance suggested. "Chicken, I was beginning to wonder if I should send someone out for you!"

Mel cast him a quick look. "I didn't think you'd worry about me, Maisy. You know what tonight is."

The woman propped bony hands on her narrow hips and harrumphed. She cast a critical eye up and down Luke. "And who would you be?"

"Maisy," Mel shifted between them, making Luke wonder if she was trying to protect the scrawny little woman, or him. "This is Luke—"

"Trahern," he supplied when she looked to him.

"An associate of Dr. Frame's," Mel went on. "Luke, Maisy Fielding. Owner of Maisy's Place."

Luke nodded at the woman, but his mind was elsewhere. *What* was tonight to Mel? The thing that had caused her to sit on the beach, weeping her heart out. "Mrs. Fielding," he said. "Jason's often said how much he enjoys staying in your cottages."

Harrumphing again, Maisy looked at Mel. Her tart demeanor visibly softened. "Are you all right?"

Mel's cheeks reddened. Luke wasn't surprised when she didn't so much as breathe in his direction. "Of course. Just a little damp. From the rain." She moistened her lips. "Luke was kind enough to lend me his jacket."

Maisy's pointed little chin turned in his direction again. "Hmm. I see. Well, thank you, Mr. Trahern, for looking out for our Mel."

"It's doctor, actually. But Luke suits me better," he added slowly, watching Mel, who had stiffened at his words. "Jason assured me there would be no problem if I took over his reservation for the week."

"Dr. Frame and his wife have been visitors here for a long time. He's never mentioned you."

If Maisy Fielding thought he would be offended by her words, she was barking up the wrong tree. Nor was it his imagination that she was most definitely drawing an invisible line. With him on one side, and her and Mel on the other. "Lydia would have Jason's head if he talked shop on their vacations," Luke countered smoothly. "He's allowed to brag about their five grandchildren all he wants, but work is forbidden."

"Why didn't they come themselves?" The question came from Mel. She was still avoiding his eyes.

"A patient," he said abruptly. It was true enough, in a manner of speaking. Only it was his patient. *Had been* his patient. "He must have gotten sidetracked, or he'd have called ahead about the switch. If you can't accommodate me, say the word. I'll make other arrangements."

"Good idea—"

"Oh, no, that won't be—"

Luke watched the two women stare at each other and wondered grimly what was behind the undercurrents running thick and heavy between them. Wondered, too, just what his boss had tossed him into, because there was little that Jason didn't do without very specific reasons.

Luke might admire the hell out of his boss, but that didn't mean he was ignorant of the man's penchant for manipulating people to suit his purposes.

"Maisy," Mel was saying softly, "the only other

empty rooms are at the Seaspray Inn, and you know he can't possibly stay there. Of course he should use Dr. Frame's reservation.''

Red curls positively vibrating with displeasure, Maisy shoved her hands into the patch pockets of her green and purple dress. ''Dr. Frame or his wife should have called about the change. I was expecting *them.*'' She huffed again, then pulled out one of her hands and extended a large key. ''I serve breakfast in the dining room between eight and nine o'clock. Don't expect room service, because we don't give it. If you miss the meal, you miss it. Whether you do or not, the rest of the day you're on your own.''

Luke took the key. He wasn't interested in food, simply a clean, dry bed. ''Thank you.''

He wouldn't have thought it possible for Maisy's eyes to narrow even more, but they did. As if she didn't quite trust his polite expression. ''The Blue Cottage,'' she finally added. ''The last one on the path from the main building. You ought to be able to find it, even in the dark.''

''Mel can show me the way.''

Mel, however, looked as if she wanted to do anything but that. ''A-all right. Yes. Of course.'' She leaned over and bussed Maisy's cheek. He overheard her soft murmur to the woman that she was ''tired anyway.''

''Between eight and nine,'' Maisy reminded, as he and Mel started off again.

If he *did* sleep, he hoped like hell it would be for about twenty-four hours straight, and Maisy's breakfast hour be hanged. As for Maisy herself, he'd be dealing with her soon enough, since that was Jason's only charge in suggesting Luke take advantage of his reservation and regroup.

Regroup. As if he'd had some small setback.

He followed Mel as they left the noise of the party behind. He watched her hair drifting around her shoulders. Moonbeams, he thought again, then shoved his hands into his pockets as he walked along, cutting off that entire area of thought. The thought embargo lasted all of fifteen minutes. He figured he'd done well, at that, considering the fingertips of one hand were tangled in the delicate hank of silky fabric in his pocket.

He pulled his hands free. "What's wrong with the Seaspray Inn?" He wasn't dying of curiosity, but at least it was a safe topic.

"Excuse me?"

"The Seaspray. You said I couldn't possibly stay there."

She looked away from him again. "It's on the other side of the island. Near Castillo Cove."

"So? Too pricey for the likes of me?"

She made a soft sound. "The fees at Seaspray are perfectly reasonable. It's just not a very popular place with visitors."

"Why not?"

She looked uncomfortable. "It's kind of barren over there," she finally said. "The people who go there are usually locals and there are only a few rooms. Even if they have a vacancy, you'd have probably been turned away. Nothing personal. But you're not a Turn." They walked a while longer in silence.

"Were they celebrating something in particular back there?"

"A birthday."

"Full of information, aren't you."

The rhythmic squishing of her sandals hesitated. "You didn't say you were a doctor."

"We didn't exactly exchange résumés down there on the sand." Full body contact, yeah. Talk, details of their respective lives—no.

"Do you specialize?"

"Yes."

When he said no more than that, she looked over her shoulder at him, never slowing her pace. "Now who is being reticent?"

"Pediatric neurosurgery."

She stumbled a little. He shot out an arm, steadying her. "A surgeon," she murmured. "Naturally."

"Something wrong with that?"

"Not if you're a child requiring neurosurgery," she said, and began walking again. "We're almost there."

Luke tilted his head back, feeling the mist on his face. The moisture didn't so much rain on him as enclose him. He blew out a long breath and cursed Jason, even though he knew his friend's motives in sending him to this place had been more altruistic than not.

"Luke? Are you coming or planning to stand in the rain until dawn?"

He slicked his hand down his face and caught up to her with two long strides. "Are you planning to stay with me until dawn?" So much for safe topics.

He heard her quick inhalation and that betraying hesitation in her squishing steps as they walked up the stone path to the inn. "You shouldn't say things like that."

"I should pretend that nothing happened."

"Isn't that the way men like it? A...good time, with no strings attached?"

"That's it." He closed his hands over her shoulders, stopping her progress, making her stand there and face him. "I don't know what the hell kind of game you're playing." It infuriated him that he'd believed she hadn't been playing anything. "And right now, I'm too far beyond pissed to care. You don't want anything more to transpire between us, fine. I'm reasonably intelligent. I get it. But don't make it sound as if all I was out for was a *good* time. Don't forget, baby, you kissed me."   .

Disgusted with himself, with everything, he let go of her and stomped up the porch steps to grab his duffel, which he'd dumped there earlier. He unzipped the side and pulled out a cheerfully wrapped package that he tossed to her as he went back down the steps. She caught it, surprised.

"That's from Jason and Lydia for Maisy's granddaughter," he said flatly. "I suspect if I give it to Maisy directly, she'll toss it in a tub of water first just to see if it explodes."

"You're exaggerating."

"Don't think so. Suspicion reached new heights with Maisy Fielding. Where is her granddaughter anyway?"

"At the party, of course. It's for her and she does have a name. April."

"Isn't it a little late for a seven-year-old to be at a

party?'' Much less a girl who was as ill as Jason had indicated.

"She wanted a grown-up party,'' Mel said. Her voice was thin. "It's not so much to ask. There are places she can rest at the community center. Lily Villanova is there. She's a relative of sorts to Maisy. She helps look after April.''

From Jason, Luke knew that Maisy had been raising April since she was a baby, after April's mother, Tessa, left the island, only to never return. There had been an exhaustive search, but she'd seemed to disappear right from the planet.

"Well, the gift is for her, April. Jase and Lydia would undoubtedly appreciate it if she actually received it.'' He stepped past Mel, heading around the side of the inn. Jason's incessant descriptions were at least proving useful now. Luke figured he could find the last cottage on the lane with no assistance. And the sooner he got away from Mel, the better.

He didn't like being an idiot any more than he liked being a failure.

"It's not you.'' Mel was following him. He looked back, just to be sure he wasn't imagining it. There she was, trotting after him, clutching the wrapped present with hands that were nearly swallowed by long leather sleeves. "Maisy's behavior. She doesn't open up easily to outsiders.''

He stopped in front of the last cottage. Lacy Queen palms bracketed the door that even in the dim light he could tell was painted a bright blue. "But she'll run guest cottages for those outsiders.''

"It's her livelihood.''

He refrained from belaboring the irony. "So that's Maisy's excuse. What's yours?"

She didn't look at him. "I don't know what you mean."

"Bull."

"You're not at all like Dr. Frame."

"No kidding." He smiled humorlessly. Luke knew for a fact that, before he'd turned to administration, Jason had possessed one of the most spectacular success records of any surgeon in the field. Until recently, Luke had been hard on Jason's heels in that regard. He doubted that Mel knew that, though. More likely, she'd taken one look at him and, without a suit and tie or scrubs, decided he didn't look the part. It wouldn't be the first time he'd been judged that way, but it had long ago ceased to matter to him. He was what he was. A rancher's grandson who'd been encouraged to follow his call.

Only now he wasn't sure about that calling at all.

He headed to the blue door and fit the old-fashioned, oversize key into the lock. The door swung inward.

"Luke."

Don't be even more monumentally stupid than you've already been, he told himself. Go inside. Shut the bloody door and go to bed. *Alone.* He dumped his duffel inside the doorway. Exhaling a long breath, he turned around to face her. She was holding out his jacket, her expression torn. "I'm sorry."

Feeling even wearier than he had been before he'd encountered Mel, he took the jacket from her. The slick lining of it was warm from her body. "For what?"

She closed her arms over her chest. ''For everything.'' Then she turned on her heel.

Luke didn't go inside until he could no longer see the glint of her pale hair and the ghostly drift of her dress through the mist.

By the time morning came, he was almost convinced he'd imagined the entire episode. But the silky strand of white-blond hair caught on the collar of his sand-encrusted jacket told him otherwise.

He took the jacket and opened the rear door of the small cottage. Outside, the morning sun was brilliant, the sky an endless blanket of brilliant blue. The air was cool and clean, and the view of the ocean spectacular.

''Paradise,'' Jason had told him.

Luke sighed. He held out the jacket and shook it hard. Sand rained down on the dry stone patio.

''I'm sorry, too,'' he murmured.

He was. He just wasn't quite sure what exactly he was the most sorry about.

Chapter 4

The light shining behind Mel's eyelids told her it was morning. Well past time to get her lethargic bones out of the cocoon offered by her bed.

She opened her eyes. They felt dry and scratchy. Probably because she'd not given them any true rest until nearly dawn. She rolled on her side, cushioning her head on her folded arm, and stared past the empty half of the bed to the alarm clock on the opposite nightstand.

Of course, her mother wouldn't call the little three-legged turquoise-painted table a nightstand. But it was enough to hold Mel's clock and a small lamp. The clock told her it was most definitely time to get herself going. Past time.

She pushed up on her elbows, wrinkling her nose at the abrasive feel of the white sheet. Even though she had showered when she'd come in, there were still a few grains of sand in her sheets. "Cracker crumbs are nothing compared to a little piece of the beach," she murmured as she pushed back the bedding and padded to the small bathroom attached to her room. She'd shower again, change the sheets, then go over to the inn and the small room there that served as an office for Maisy's Place.

If she was lucky, she'd be able to avoid Dr. Luke Trahern altogether.

The pipes rattled when she flipped on the shower. But the water came out in a strong enough spray, rapidly filling the dinky bathroom with steam. Mel only wished she could blot out the memory of the previous night as easily as the fog blotted out the mirror above the sink.

She tugged off the faded T-shirt she'd worn to sleep in and stepped under the shower. The heat slowly worked its way into her sore muscles. Mel didn't want to remember just exactly why she felt tender and tired, but the reason still sat there in her mind, large as life. How could it not? She hadn't been with a man since Jonathan.

Mel ignored the whispered thought and blindly snatched up the bottle of shampoo. It was handmade on the island, but just then she had no appreciation whatsoever for the calming scent. Ten minutes later, her wet hair woven back into a French braid that reached halfway down her back, she was on her way to her office.

Of course, the first person she encountered was the one individual she'd hoped to avoid. Her footsteps faltered as she turned the corner and saw Luke leaning against the wall next to her office door, She didn't even have an opportunity to turn tail and run because he immediately spotted her and straightened from his indolent slouch.

There was nothing indolent about his hooded gaze, however, when he focused on her and she felt the sting of color heat her cheeks. She fell back on her role as manager with no small amount of desperation. "Is the cottage to your satisfaction?"

"There's no phone."

"I'm sorry, I thought you knew. None of the cottages are wired for phones. But there is always someone on hand to answer the main line in the inn, in case you're expecting a call. And of course it's available for your use whenever you need. Unfortunately cell phones are useless out here. No signal. Is, um, everything else to your comfort?"

"Yes."

When it became apparent that he wasn't going to add anything else, that he wasn't going to ease the awkwardness between them with some sort of idle chitchat about the weather or the incredible color of the ocean, she stepped past him and entered the office, harboring a fantasy that he'd go along his way.

But she knew he wouldn't. For why else would he have been standing outside her office if not to see her?

She moved behind her desk, setting aside the small basket filled with two enormous apricot-walnut muffins. Every morning, before the crack of dawn, Maisy prepared the fresh muffins for the guests, saving two for Mel to begin her day. If April was feeling up to it, she was charged with the task of sneaking into the office to set the basket front and center on Mel's white-washed oak desk.

The apricot-walnut muffin fairies. April always giggled over the "mystery" of how the muffins came to appear on Mel's desk each morning. Mel would swallow glass before she'd unveil her knowledge of that particular pleasure for the child.

Sitting down was not an option. Being seated with Luke looming tall and brooding over her desk was definitely *not* the way to go. So she stood, and tried not to fidget with the stapler or the muffin basket.

"Are you all right?"

"Of course."

"Are you sure?"

"Why wouldn't I be?" She cringed at her sharp tone.

He looked at her and her cheeks went even hotter. She wished he would get to the point of his visit and be on his way. He was tall and masculine and filling up her small office in a way that made her feel vaguely panicked. As if she might do something stupid again. Like baldly throwing herself at him one more time.

His lips twisted, and she wondered if he'd read her mind, or if his thoughts were as unwanted as her own.

"We didn't use anything," he said.

Mel nearly choked. She couldn't even pretend she didn't know of what he spoke, because the way they'd behaved was, well, too…large…in her thoughts to ignore. "It's okay." Her voice was faint.

"You're on the Pill, then."

"Well, no, but—"

His eyebrow lifted. "No?"

She wanted him out of her office. She wanted him off the island. Then, maybe, she could stop the unfamiliar sensations that curled inside her. "You needn't worry," she assured flatly.

He was still, his attention never wavering from her face. "I'm a doctor," he said. "I made one mistake already with you, having unprotected sex."

"Please, don't—"

"I'm not likely to make another mistake and act as if it didn't happen." He rolled right over her embarrassed protests. "There are health issues at stake, not just the matter of pregnancy."

Forget the home-court advantage. She needed to sit, after all. "I can't get pregnant." Not only was the notion terrifying, it was really impossible. "The past had proven that. I don't have any dreaded diseases. So can we please end this conversation now?"

He looked as if he had plenty more to say on the matter. She nearly oozed off her chair in relief when he didn't speak.

He reached out and plucked one of the muffins from the basket. "Do you mind?"

As long as he took it and went, she'd gladly give him both muffins. "Help yourself."

He didn't go, however. He leisurely consumed half the muffin, looking perfectly at home. "I need a favor," he finally said.

"What kind of favor?" With any other guest, she'd have immediately offered whatever assistance she could provide. With Luke, however, she couldn't seem to find her way back from the person who'd buried her grief with him on a windswept beach, to the manager of Maisy's Place. He wasn't just a guest and she couldn't pretend otherwise. Though she was certainly going to try.

"So suspicious." Another bite and the muffin was gone. "Dr. Frame seems to think that Maisy's granddaughter should be evaluated."

Mel's heart squeezed. April Fielding was a joy in all of their lives. But April was dying. "You'll have to talk to Maisy about that."

"I have."

"When? It's still early."

"In the kitchen. She was baking." His gaze drifted to the other muffin. As far as Mel could tell, there was no dissatisfaction in his expression. But she didn't need there to be any to know how that particular conversation must have turned out.

"Maisy won't allow it," she predicted flatly. "I could have told you that before you bothered her." A part of her mind wondered if he'd gotten any sleep at all if he'd been bothering Maisy during her preferred baking time.

"Which is where the favor comes in," he said mildly. "Everyone around here I've talked to this morning says you and Maisy are close, that you're very fond of April. Talk Maisy into it. I can't get near the girl without Maisy's consent. Without her cooperation."

No matter what Mel's personal feelings were, she respected Maisy's position. She might not agree, but she certainly did understand. She knew, only too well, how much the little girl had already endured at the hands of the medical profession. "Maisy is April's legal guardian. She's devoted to her."

"So devoted she won't let the girl be seen by anyone but the doctor who's here on the island."

He couldn't have been more wrong, but it wasn't Mel's place to divulge Maisy's business. "Maisy trusts Dr. Hugo. He's served the Turns for decades."

"There's no hospital here. Dr. Frame said the clinic isn't remotely equipped to handle a case like April's. And regardless of equipment or lack of it, no matter the longevity of a doctor-patient relationship, any medical professional will tell you that second opinions are never unwarranted."

Unless that medical professional believes he's the next thing to God. Mel stifled the bitter thought. "If Dr. Frame has such a strong conviction on this, he could have spoken to Maisy himself, on any number of occasions."

"He's not actively practicing."

"I know that. But Maisy has known the Frames for many years. She does respect him."

"And she neither knows nor respects me."

"Don't put words in my mouth."

"Even if they're true."

She felt rather like a child summoned to the principal's office. The fact that he was right made it no more palatable. "Maisy doesn't know you," she allowed.

His expression didn't change. But the air between them was suddenly charged and she felt the impact of his deep blue gaze. Her spine straightened in defense against the ripples that skittered along it.

"Not like you do," he said.

Denial leaped to her lips, but the words stalled. Did she know him? At all? Had she imagined the connection she'd felt last night on the beach? Was it merely wishful thinking that what had occurred had had nothing to do with sex and everything to do with one despairing human reaching out for another?

Or was she merely trying to justify her positively outrageous behavior?

A pain set up a lively beat in her temple. "If Maisy had wanted Dr. Frame's medical opinion, she'd have asked for it."

"That's your answer. You're not going to help April."

"I'm not going to help manipulate my friend just so you can feel the high-and-mighty surgeon," she said flatly. "Dr. Frame surely knew better than to interfere."

"Dr. Frame has April's best interests in mind."

"Meaning that April's grandmother doesn't?" She struggled against her rising temper.

"Now who's putting words in someone's mouth?" He flattened his palms on the edge of her desk and leaned forward. "I don't know what you've got against surgeons or if it's just something about last night and me that you don't want to face. But I came here because Jason asked me to see what I could do. I specialize in pediatric cases. Maybe he considers April worth the interference."

"So, you're looking to win brownie points with him. What's at stake? A promotion of some sort? A partnership with Dr. Frame?" She knew the moment the words found life that she'd gone too far. Disagreeing with him was one thing, deliberately insulting him an-other. "I'm sorry."

He'd straightened from the desk, his eyes unread-able. "The person you should be apologizing to is April Fielding." Then he turned on his heel and walked away.

Mel sagged back against her chair, swiveling around to face the window behind her desk. The view beyond was the type that sold glossy travel magazines by the thousands—vivid green palms swaying in a balmy breeze, ripples of pristine white sand disappearing into a calm azure ocean. In her mind's eye, however, all she saw was the gleam of a small casket draped in tulips being slowly lowered into the cold, hard ground.

Sighing, she left her office and went in search of Maisy.

Luke found the office of Dr. Hugo easily enough. He'd headed up the only road and stopped when he came to the pink-and-blue square house with a weather-beaten wooden sign hanging from a rusty metal hook that read Doctor.

The front door was wide-open, obviously taking ad-vantage of the morning breeze that had the collection of wind chimes hanging over the porch jangling in cheerful harmony. He ducked his head under the chimes and went inside. There was no receptionist, no patients sitting in the cluster of chairs situated around an oval coffee table. The surface of the table was al-most obscured by outdated entertainment magazines.

If not for the wind chimes, the place would have been as silent as a tomb. He walked down the central hallway of the clinic. It was obvious that, at one point, the place had been a residence. The doors that opened off either side of the hallway had undoubtedly been bedrooms. Now they were small exam rooms that were more on the barren side than the well equipped.

He continued down the short hall to the door at the end of it, and knocked. There was no answer, and he opened it. Instead of an interior office, however, the door opened to the outside again. He focused on the white-haired man sitting before an upturned barrel covered with cards in a game of solitaire. "Dr. Hugo?"

The other man barely gave him a glance. The unlit cigar in his mouth slid from one corner to the other as he frowned at his display of cards. "You sick?"

"No."

The answer earned him another glance. "I don't got none of that Viagra stuff."

For the first time that morning, Luke felt a stab of humor. "I'm not looking for any."

"Tourists," the other man said, flipping up another three cards and shaking his head critically, whether for the tourists or the cards, Luke couldn't tell.

"Every week one of you comes looking for Viagra," the man went on. "There isn't a single dose on Turnabout."

"Only thing I'm looking for is April Fielding's history," Luke said, and stuck out his hand. "Luke Trahern. I'm an associate of Jason Frame. He spoke with you the last time he visited Turnabout."

The old man adjusted his cigar again, took another considering look at Luke, then brusquely returned the handshake. "Maisy doesn't like strangers poking into her granddaughter's business."

"She's protective of her grandchild. It's understandable. But you shared April's prognosis with Dr. Frame."

"Professional courtesy. And Maisy about boiled my head for chowder when she found out," he added with a grimace. He chewed his cigar a moment, looking Luke up and down. "April has a brain tumor. Nobody on this isle wants that child to die. But it is gonna happen."

"It could happen later rather than sooner," Luke said. "There are some techniques we've developed that—"

"There's always some new technique. Some new drug protocol, some new miracle. April is seven years old now. She's had her condition since she was a toddler. She's already outlived everyone's expectations by several years."

Frustration tangoed with anger. "That's defeatist. All I want is to look over her history. She's very young for atypical meningioma."

The other man's eyes were a pale, faded green. His years were mapped in the wrinkles on his weathered face. "You get Maisy to agree, and my files are your files." His expression was clear. He knew that Maisy wouldn't acquiesce.

"I'll hold you to that," Luke said evenly. He wasn't used to failing, and he'd had too bitter a taste of it lately. His skills were in the O.R. At least they had been. Given his go-round with Maisy Fielding that morning, he seriously doubted his ability to change

Maisy's mind, and wondered why in hell Jason had thought he could.

The cigar shifted corners again. "Should've asked for Viagra. Would have been easier to produce." The old doctor turned back to his solitaire game.

Luke could see the other man had said all he intended to. He left and walked back down the long road, past several flower fields that undulated in waves of vibrant colors. He slowed and watched. It was idyllic, he thought.

Idyllic and impossible to enjoy. Because once again, he was failing those who needed him the most.

April Fielding was only the latest name on a list that had grown too long.

Chapter 5

Six months later

Mel stood on the beach, watching the setting sun. In the four years since she'd come to Turnabout, she'd never tired of the sight. Today, though, she was even more grateful than usual for the descent of evening because it meant the air would finally start to cool. The summer heat had never bothered her as much as it did this year.

She tilted back her head, letting the breeze blow her hair away from her face. The air whispered along her neck, sliding up her nape. She sighed. Closed her eyes. Red orbs shone against the inside of her eyelids but all her mind saw was a cloudy, moonlit night.

She opened her eyes. Thinking about Luke Trahern—*Dr.* Luke Trahern—served no useful purpose. He'd left the island six months ago, after staying only a few days. There was no reason to think she'd see him again. There was no reason he'd want to see her. She sighed again.

No reason.

She'd been telling herself that for several months now. She still believed it. Didn't she? She was only thinking about him now, because she was out here on the beach where they'd…they'd…

What they'd done had been madness. Aside from marrying Jonathan when she'd been a silly young college student with stars in her eyes and romance clouding her good sense, what she'd done with Luke had been the single most foolish action in all the thirty-one years of her life.

Her legs ached. She'd been on her feet too long. She sat down, tucking her skirt around her knees. But even her seated position reminded her of that night. Because she'd been seated just like this when Luke had come across her.

Why had *this* year been so different than the previous ones? Maisy gave a birthday party for April every year on that day, after all, though this was the first time it had been held in the evening. Mel had left the celebration because she hadn't been able to bear the festivity one moment longer. And she'd sought solitude on the beach as she did every year on that particular night, hoping for the peace to get her through to the next morning. To survive yet another year.

Another year without Nicky.

She swallowed and covered her face with her hands. Nicky's loss was a constant ache inside her. One that had become more bearable as the weeks, months, passed. But on that particular night, each year, the ache couldn't be contained. It continued to find its way, front and center, until it threatened to consume her sanity, her soul.

But this year, there had been someone *else* on her beach with her. Someone who hadn't let her cry alone.

Mel pressed a fist to her lips, the memory far too vivid for her peace of mind. He'd been a stranger, and she'd known it immediately. If he weren't, he'd have been back in the community center, raising the roof with music and voice, food and drink, along with every other resident of Turnabout—most of whom she knew at least by sight if not by name. He wouldn't have been out there walking along what she'd come to consider *her* patch of ivory white sand, where she could let the wind blow around her, through her, soothing away the pain that writhed inside her.

There was no way to soften the truth. Regardless of the circumstances, of her state of mind that night, she'd thrown herself at Luke Trahern, and he'd well and truly caught her. At least for a few hours.

Then he was gone, and she could hardly blame him. Neither she nor Maisy had gone out of their way to make him feel welcome. Regret was a familiar taste for Mel, though she'd worked hard over the past few years to keep from having a steady diet of it. But she did regret treating Luke the way she had. Before they'd slept together on the beach, and afterward.

Pushing those thoughts away, her gaze slid along the horizon. There was old Diego and his ugly but sturdy craft, heading back out to the mainland for his last run of the day.

Her legs were beginning to cramp. She pushed to her feet, wincing a little. It was time she got started on dinner for Maisy and April. And these days, the walk from her favorite beach perch back to the inn took a bit longer than it used to.

She tugged a little on her dress and turned to head back. All thoughts of cold soups, chicken salad or sliced turkey wrap, went right out of her head, though, at the man standing several yards off.

For a moment she actually believed her thoughts had conjured his image, as adrenaline, elation, and plain old shock swept through her.

But the screech of a seagull behind her, the drone of an engine somewhere up on the road, the soft hiss of water sliding over sand told her she was quite lucid.

Luke was definitely there.

His tall body seemed intensely still. There was no pretending that he hadn't seen her. She was the only one on the beach. Except for him. "Luke."

Sunlight glinted on his blinding white polo shirt. She couldn't see his expression. But she could imagine it. There was no reason for her to stand there like a guilty criminal in the eye of her executioner. Yet she couldn't make her feet move one inch in the soft sand beneath her.

She watched him push his hands into the front pockets of his baggy khaki-colored shorts. Evidently his feet didn't suffer the same lack of superiority over the sand as hers, because he slowly closed the distance between them.

Then Mel could see his expression all too clearly.

She swallowed. Feeling nervous, foolish, damnably *caught.* Jonathan had often stared at her in the same way. As if he could intimidate her into speaking first whenever they were at an impasse of one sort or another. Which, admittedly, had been most of the time.

The one who speaks first loses. The thought hovered

in her mind. With Jonathan, she'd known exactly what was at stake. With Luke? She wasn't at all sure she could bear to find out.

His lips were tight, rimmed by a thin line of white. A muscle jerked in his jaw. She had the brief notion again of walking away, but dismissed it immediately.

"What are you doing here?" Lose or not, she couldn't bear the silence another moment.

"Is it mine?"

She tightened her knees, painfully aware that she might have swayed. She almost pressed her hand protectively to her abdomen, and only sheer willpower kept her hands at her sides. "I don't know what you mean."

His laugh was short and totally devoid of humor. He stepped forward and, before she could finish drawing in a shocked breath, wrapped his hand in the loose, gauzy folds of her dress, tightening it against her obviously pregnant body. "Is that baby mine?" The words were slow. Torturous. Furious.

She yanked back from him, uncaring that he still held her dress, that if he hadn't suddenly let go, she'd have torn the delicate fabric beyond repair. Then she did cross her arms over herself, and if it betrayed defensiveness or protectiveness, that was too bad. "This baby is mine," she said flatly. And God help her, she was barely able to cope with that fact, much less this man appearing again.

Luke's fingers curled as he studied Mel's fierce expression. He wanted to reach for her again. To do what? Shake her? Kiss her? He wanted a reaction from her. Anything other than the pale, shocked stare she'd had since she spotted him. "And a convenient way to get yourself a doctor for a husband," he goaded.

She gaped. "What?"

"It's hardly an original method, but it's effective enough. That baby is mine. I won't let it be born a bastard." *Not like I was,* he thought, wondering where his famed patience had gone.

"The last thing I want is a husband who's a doctor." Her voice was sharp. "And if I'd known *that* about you before, I'd never have—"

"Tussled in the sand with the likes of me?" He deliberately unlocked his jaw. She was right, of course, and he'd known it even as the accusation came out of his mouth. He hadn't told her what he was any more than she'd given him her life history before they'd climbed inside each other's skin that night. "You told me pregnancy wasn't possible." Information that should have been discussed *before* they burned sand into glass.

"I thought it wasn't."

Which told him exactly nothing and made him want to know everything. "You should have contacted me," he said.

Her expression didn't change. Or course, she hadn't admitted to anything, either.

Didn't matter. The moment Luke had seen the swirling blue fabric of Mel's dress blow against her otherwise slender silhouette, he'd known. She was pregnant. The baby was his. He knew it with every breath in his body. Yet she hadn't bothered with the tiny detail of letting him know. The betrayal of it bit hard. But he'd deal with that later.

She was still silent. Her eyes wouldn't meet his and he stifled a sigh, anger a hard knot deep down inside him. She looked like another gust of wind might just blow her over. And it was patently obvious that she hadn't expected him. He supposed he could thank Maisy for that, because the ornery woman had expected him. He'd spoken to her himself. Hell, she'd directed him to Mel's whereabouts when he'd checked in.

He put his hands back in his pockets again. "You should get off your feet."

Her eyebrows shot up. "I beg your pardon?"

"Beg all you want," he said evenly. "Your ankles are swelling. You need to get your feet elevated."

Her cheeks went red. "Well, I don't *need* anyone telling me what I need. I'm perfectly capable of watching out for myself."

Definitely a sore point. "Like you clearly felt no *need* to contact me with the happy news."

Her brown eyes flickered. "Luke, what are you... why are you here?"

"Mel!"

They both jerked at the hail, and Luke swallowed his response. What he was doing on Turnabout had nothing to do with the shock of finding her pregnant and everything to do with the mess he'd created.

A golden-skinned young man skidded in the sand as he stopped next to Mel. "Maisy's been looking for you." His words were for Mel, but his frankly suspicious gaze was all for Luke. Mel had captured her hair again in one hand and Luke felt another shaft of hot remembrance.

"Thanks, Tomas."

"I brought a cart."

Sure enough, there was a lime-green golf cart parked some distance away. Luke was more interested, though, in the flicker of relief that crossed Mel's drawn features.

Without looking Luke's way, she mumbled an excuse and began walking toward the cart. Tomas Duran looked half Luke's age. He was definitely younger than Mel, but the protective stance the man took as he walked beside Mel was loud and clear. As clear as the unhappy look he gave her when she stopped halfway to the cart and looked back at Luke.

"Coming?"

A smart man would sit back, let his emotions cool and examine the situation with tactical precision. A smart man wouldn't have been allowing his life to slip through his fingers for the past half year. "Yeah," he said. "I'm coming."

The fact that he took some satisfaction from the flare of panic in her eyes told him how much better it would have been to take the smart route. But he'd apparently given up that path when he'd taken Mel into his arms with no concern or thought to consequences until it was too late.

He stepped up and sat on the rear-facing bench, well aware of the worried looks Mel surreptitiously sent him as Tomas took the wheel and the cart lurched over the sand. When the tires hit the sunbaked tarmac, though, they made short work of the distance back to the inn.

A small crowd had gathered on the neatly trimmed grass in front of the main building and Luke swallowed an oath when Mel jumped from the cart before it had even come to a stop. He caught up to her as she crouched down beside a young man, and Luke silently absorbed the way she pressed her hand comfortingly to the guy's brown-skinned shoulder.

"What happened?"

Dr. Hugo looked up at Luke over the prone man. "Ah, Leo Vega here thought he'd work on the roof without benefit of a ladder. Don't think whoever he was trying to impress saw fit to hang around when he fell on his butt.'' He waved his hand over Leo's swollen ankle. "Got a healthy sprain and a bruised ego, but he'll live.''

Leo groaned and folded his arm over his eyes as a chuckle worked through the small crowd. Mel's head was bent close to Leo's as she murmured something.

Leo didn't look quite as young as Tomas and the instinct to pull her away from the guy was a foreign and unwelcome one. Luke studied Leo's ankle until the urge passed. "He needs an X ray," he told Hugo.

"Think so, eh?" Hugo's cigar—unlit as always—rolled from one corner of his mouth to the other. He looked back down at Leo. "Guess you know what to do, son.''

Leo groaned, nodded. Somebody produced an ancient wood-and-canvas stretcher, Leo was loaded up by his friends, and they trotted off down the road, laughing and poking fun at Leo's clumsiness.

"That boy's gotten into more fixes from pulling some stunt to impress a pretty girl," Hugo said, shaking his head as he pushed to his feet. "But he's been a handyman for Maisy since he was a schoolboy, and she doesn't seem to mind the eye he casts over the guests as long as he keeps his hands to himself. Mel, I'll get the info for the insurance to you later.''

Luke rose too and, ignoring the tight-lipped look she cast him, helped Mel to her feet. "Are they taking him to your clinic?''

Hugo shook his head. "No point.''

"Leo lives with his sister, Jane." Mel put in, moving her arm away from his hand. "She'll take care of him until he's ready to come back to work.''

"You look like you swallowed something still wriggling," Hugo said, and there was only one word Luke could think of to describe the man's expression as he looked from Luke to Mel—*crafty.*

For a moment, just a brief moment, Hugo reminded Luke of his grandfather. But it was enough to let a swell of undefined emotion join the flood already filling him every time he looked at Mel.

Every time he looked at the swell of the child growing inside her. His child.

Mel must have seen that look of Hugo's, too, because she suddenly cleared her throat and spoke. "I have to get Maisy and April's dinner," she announced, and turned on her heel and hurried away. Her dress fluttered like a song around her slender legs and her hair danced around her shoulders as she moved. Lithe. Graceful.

But there was no mistaking what she was doing. Fleeing.

Chapter 6

"You knew Luke Trahern was coming, I take it," Mel said as she slid the heavy tray she'd carried from the inn's kitchen onto the table in Maisy's cottage.

Maisy's thin fingers toyed with her narrow glass of fresh lemonade. "His money is as green as anyone else's."

"You've turned away other guests with plenty of green stuff," Mel said as she laid out the meal for her friends, then sat down in the third chair to join them for dinner. Tonight her appetite was nil. "You weren't at all pleased when he showed up instead of Dr. Frame earlier this year. I thought you'd dance a jig when he left only a few days after he'd arrived."

Maisy's lips tightened. "Maybe I can't afford to do that anymore—turn away paying customers."

"What are you talking about? Maisy's Place is doing very well. Occupancy is the highest it's ever been."

"What's 'occupancy'?" April's green eyes were bright and curious, completely belying the fact that she was nearly blind.

Maisy reached over and gently brushed April's dark blond curls away from her ivory forehead. The ringlets promptly sprang back into place. April was having a good day today, which tended to put everything else into perspective. The annoyance that had been budding inside Mel since Luke had found her on the beach trickled away, leaving her feeling tired, and mostly confused.

"It's how many beds we've got filled at the inn, chicken."

"How come you call me 'n' Mel 'chicken'?"

"How come you're so full of questions today?"

April shrugged. Then she forked another chunk of mango into her little bowlike mouth. "I wanna learn everything in the whole world," she said around her food.

Maisy's smile looked a little strained at the edges. Mel leaned across the table, studying April seriously. She'd learned early on to not act as if April's sight was impaired, for the child had an uncanny sense of being able to decipher expressions despite her challenge. "*Everything?* That's a whole lot. Then there'd be no surprises left."

April seemed to consider that as she plowed her way hungrily through her meal. At that moment, nobody would ever imagine the child was seriously, desperately ill. "I like surprises," the little girl said after a while. "Good surprises, I mean. Bad surprises are just yucky."

Mel smiled then pointedly looked over at Maisy. "I hear you on that one, pumpkin."

Maisy raised her chin, looking not the least bit defensive. Mel didn't know what she'd expected. It wasn't as if she and Maisy had ever sat down and discussed how Mel came to be pregnant. She owed her sanity to Maisy, but even with *her* Mel hadn't been able to discuss what had happened on the beach. But that didn't mean Maisy couldn't have her suspicions.

"When did he make his reservation?"

"Two weeks ago."

Mel absorbed that. "You put him in the Blue Cottage." The cottage that Maisy had abruptly "closed" for renovations two weeks earlier. Renovations that hadn't yet begun, a fact that Mel had blamed on the sometimes fluid definition of time the Turns exhibited. Now she realized there were no renovations to be done, at all.

"Grammy, can I be excused?"

Maisy gave her permission and April scrambled off the chair, took a moment to find her balance, then scampered out the door into the enclosed garden and play area where she plopped down on the grass with her collection of toys.

Mel watched Maisy watch April and her heart squeezed in empathy. She didn't know what Maisy was up to, but she knew she didn't have the heart to probe. Not when Maisy looked every bit as tired as Mel felt, and certainly not when Maisy only wanted to share every precious moment she and her granddaughter had together.

"Go on out with her," Mel said gently. "I'll clean up here."

"You do too much, chicken." Maisy sighed and patted Mel's hand before standing. "You're like my daughter was when she was pregnant with April. Always doing, doing. Going, going. She should've had someone taking care of her when she was big with a baby, too." Not giving Mel a chance to respond to that, she slipped out the door and joined April.

Mel leaned back in the chair, her hand resting on the restless movements of the baby. A vision of an auburn-headed boy swam into her thoughts and she banished it before the wave of pain could accompany it. Pushing to her feet, she returned the dishes to the tray and propped one edge of it on her hip to carry back to the main building where the kitchen was located.

She could hear April's chatter and giggles and Maisy's lower voice as she let herself out of their home and headed to the path, turning left. She didn't dare look down the path the other way to the blue-doored cottage that lay at the end of it.

"Are you done avoiding me?"

Mel quailed inwardly at the hard look in Luke's eyes when she stopped beside the small table he was occupying in the sun-drenched dining room the next morning. The fact that she *had* been avoiding him made her cowardice even more abhorrent. She wasn't a doormat, she reminded herself firmly. Not anymore. It had taken her years to work the footprints out of her spine.

"I want an apology." She got out the words she'd rehearsed half the sleepless night before.

His slashing eyebrows skyrocketed. "What? You're the one who—"

"You accused me of angling for a husband. I wasn't. I'm *not*. The last thing I want is a husband—trust me. And I want an apology."

A muscle in his jaw ticked. But his voice was smooth. "All right. I apologize."

Surprise hit her. She hadn't truly expected him to do anything of the sort. Neither Jonathan nor her father would have.

"Now, would you sit down? Please?"

She swallowed and slipped into the waiting chair. "Is breakfast to your satisfaction?"

His lips twisted. "We're going to discuss scrambled eggs and fresh fruit?"

"The, um, the food is all from local sources. Eggs are from a small farm here that provides most of our dairy. And you've undoubtedly seen the citrus grove beyond the Blue Cottage. And of course, the mango and papaya—I see you tried those already. We offer lunch and dinner now, too, during the busier summer season. George Glass is a great chef. Maisy hired him a few months ago. If you join us, the seafood salad is very popular—"

"I can read the menu myself." He rested his arms on the small circular table and leaned forward. "And I don't want to talk about food unless it pertains to whether or not you've been eating properly."

She pressed her lips together, her heartbeat skittering around. She had no intention of telling him that ordinarily her appetite rivaled a horse's. At least it had until the previous day when he'd shockingly turned up on the beach. Dr. Hugo had warned her that she needed to watch her eating because she was gaining so quickly.

When she thought her voice might be remotely steady, she finally spoke. "My diet is none of your concern."

"Really. And that baby is none of my concern, either, I suppose."

A knot formed in her throat. So much for thinking he'd be put off by her demand for an apology. "No."

His hair was even longer than it had been six months earlier. Even more shaggy and more…inviting to her traitorous fingers. But when he lifted one eyebrow at her statement, he looked like a dark angel, come to punish her for her sins.

"No what? It's none of my concern, or no, it is of my concern."

His small table had originally been set for two. She focused on straightening the unused knife with the unused fork and ignored his tight question. She'd have to talk with the wait staff. The unused setting should have been removed. "I'm not going to intercede with Maisy for you about April."

"Did I ask you to?"

"You did before."

"And it didn't work," he said.

Mel chewed the inside of her lower lip. She *had* gone to Maisy that morning after he'd showed up in her office. And Maisy had done exactly what Mel had expected her to do. Refused to put her granddaughter through yet another grueling round of tests that had a ninety-nine-point-nine percent chance of giving the same exact results as all the others.

"If not about April, then why *are* you here?"

"For a vacation, of course. Isn't that what most everyone is here for when they visit Turnabout?"

Something in his tone made her look at him. He wasn't conventionally handsome. He was simply too intense. And the kindness he'd exhibited that night six months earlier seemed long gone. Still, looking at him made her stomach hollow out, reminding her that his touch had been like none other. "You're missing the carefree look of our usual tourists," she countered.

His glance dropped to her basketball-size tummy. The grooves in his hard cheek deepened. "Imagine that."

She didn't for a moment believe that she had anything to do with his purpose for coming to Turnabout. He hadn't notified her that he was coming, after all. His communication had been strictly with Maisy. And Maisy—for reasons that thoroughly escaped Mel—had chosen to keep it to herself. Unless Maisy really did suspect he'd had something to do with Mel's current state.

"Turnabout is pretty quiet for a vacation destination," she said. "There are more sights and activities on Catalina Island. And it's closer to the mainland. It's far easier to reach, more shuttle services. There's even a helicopter shuttle."

"Better not let the tourist board of Turnabout hear you." His voice was bland. "One would think you're trying to send customers to the competition."

"Catalina is hardly the competition. It's easily twice

the size of Turnabout. It's a beautiful island. Avalon—''

''I've been there,'' he cut her off. ''Two months ago, in fact. I took a weekend there.''

Mel swallowed. Somehow she had the distinct impression that he hadn't gone alone. And the thought of that was rather more disturbing than she wanted to acknowledge. Just because she and Luke had done something foolishly dangerous together didn't mean she had any right whatsoever to be interested in how he conducted his life. Or with whom.

The baby fluttered inside her and she shifted in the iron chair. Her back was hurting. She was hardly comfortable anymore, and she still had three months to go. ''H-how are Dr. Frame and his wife?''

Luke eyed the antsy woman across from him and wondered what she'd say if he told her the answer that sprang to mind. *Thoroughly disgusted with me.* ''They're fine.'' He smiled, though he felt no humor. ''They're expecting another grandchild in a few months.''

Mel's smoky lashes fell, hiding her eyes. Dark eyes, as soft and engulfing as velvet, which had haunted his thoughts for months no matter how many other women he'd seen. There'd been plenty, too. One had accompanied him on that abysmal Santa Catalina weekend. And, despite them all, he hadn't been able to keep his thoughts off this much more obscure island where a young woman with sad eyes had touched something inside him.

Belinda had stomped out on him after Catalina when it became apparent that he had no intention of taking their casual relationship to another level, calling him more names than he'd heard in years.

He should never have gotten involved with her in the first place. Even though she was a successful woman in her own right, she was still a member of the Conroy family—one of Sunquest's most generous benefactors. And the whole lot of them were more than a little disenchanted with Luke.

He didn't much care what anybody thought of him, but he did know their money was sorely needed to continue the work at Sunquest. Children from the world over depended on the clinic's services. And with Luke out of the way for a while, maybe Jason could repair the damage and coax more money from the Conroys' coffers.

"How nice for the Frames," Mel was saying. "I know they're thoroughly devoted to their grandchildren. They talk about them a lot whenever they visit Turnabout. Mrs. Frame carries around dozens of pictures of them in her purse. She's obviously very proud of them."

"What about *your*—" the word sat bitter on his tongue "—baby's grandparents? Is this their first grandchild? Their tenth? Or are you pretending that *your* baby doesn't have grandparents any more than it has a father?"

She looked as if he'd slapped her. He let out a rough breath, but couldn't bring himself to apologize. She was the one who'd kept silent about her pregnancy.

"I haven't talked to my parents in four years," she said after a moment. Her voice was brittle and her movements stiff as she pushed back the chair. She hurried away from the table as if the devil were biting at the hem of her pale green dress twining around her slender ankles.

Luke looked around the open patio that served as a dining room.

Get out of here and don't come back until you've got your head together, Luke. Jason's words swam in his thoughts.

His "vacation" was enforced. Luke could be irritated about it, aggravated and thoroughly, royally pissed. But the truth of it was Luke hadn't been doing anything good at home. He hadn't been for months. Not since before he'd visited Turnabout the first time and found Mel.

After all, what good was a surgeon who couldn't bring himself to pick up a scalpel for fear of killing another patient?

Chapter 7

Mel might have walked off on him, but Luke considered their conversation far from over. His career might be on the skids, but he wasn't going to let his personal life head any further south than it already had.

He found her in her office, looking uncommonly still where she sat in the chair behind the plain desk, gazing out the window behind it. ''There was nowhere else I wanted to go,'' he said quietly.

Her sixties-era swivel desk chair squeaked when she slowly turned to face him. Her expression was wary. And he felt like a devil because he'd caused it.

''I beg your pardon?''

''You asked why I was here.''

The corners of her lips lifted in a forced smile. ''I help run Maisy's Place,'' she reminded. ''More or less. I merely wanted to know so I could assist in arranging activities for you. If you wanted to scuba dive, or sail. Fish. Horseback ride. That sort of thing.''

He sat in the lone straight chair in front of her desk. "Liar."

Color bloomed in her cheeks and her eyes sparked. "I don't make a habit of lying."

He nodded. "I believe you. You're not very good at it."

Her lips tightened. "I think you should go."

"And if I don't?"

"Then *I'll* leave."

"And I'll come after you."

She blinked. "Is...that some sort of threat?"

"A promise."

"Why does that not comfort me?"

He leaned forward, resting his elbows on her desk. "I couldn't forget you."

She pressed back against her chair, her eyes widening. "I—what? Don't say things like that."

"Why not? It's true. I couldn't sleep at night without thinking about you." He watched her face flush. "I couldn't wake up without thinking about you."

"So, we had...great sex," she blurted out in a low voice, pushing to her feet, looking as if she was ready to run for the mainland. "*That* is what you thought about, and we both know it."

"It wasn't sex."

Her lips parted. "Oh, please. How did I get like *this* then?" Her mouth snapped shut and she stared at him.

Silence filled the room.

Even though he'd already been sure of it, her admission still rocked through him. His throat tightened.

"It was more than sex," he said. Great sex. Phenomenal sex. "We both needed something that night. Something we wouldn't have found with anyone else."

She looked panicked, now, color riding high on her cheeks. "You're romanticizing."

"You're telling me you haven't thought something similar? Not once during all the nights since?"

"No."

"I told you that you weren't a good liar."

"This must be quite a disappointment to you," she said, angling her body to move through the narrow space between her desk and the wall.

When she got bigger—and she would over the course of the next several weeks—she wouldn't even be able to fit through there, he thought.

"After my behavior last time, you probably expected a far more…entertaining…vacation. How disappointing for you. Instead of an easy lay, you found a thoroughly unattractive pregnant woman."

The tip of her nose was pink and her eyes were wet. He tamped down the anger that coursed through him and caught her wrist as she tried to step by him. He knew what was bugging him, but he was damned to figure out what was tormenting her. Other than the obvious, that was. "Stop."

She didn't look at him and he stood, very aware of the swell of their child beneath the soft fabric of her thin dress. He was also painfully aware of the thrust of her breasts and the scent of her barely golden skin, her sunshine-kissed hair.

"First of all, I didn't come to Turnabout *expecting* anything. I didn't have anywhere else to go. Secondly, there's nothing in the least bit easy about you. I never thought there was and I still don't.'' Even if he was struggling with the fact that if he hadn't come back to Turnabout, he was pretty certain she'd have kept him in the dark about her pregnancy. ''And lastly, you need to look in a mirror, honey, 'cause there's nothing unattractive about you.''

His voice was low, his words all the more fierce because of it. But one statement struck Mel far more than the others. And she trembled, because no matter how badly she wanted to pretend she had no involvement with this man, part of her silently screamed otherwise. ''What do you mean you didn't have anywhere else to go?''

His dark brows drew together. ''Marry me.''

Mel stared at him, her question lost in the gale of shock at his. ''What?''

''We're having a baby together. What do you plan to do when the baby comes? Have it here on the island? Go to a hospital in San Diego—make the crossing while you're in labor? What about after? You want to raise him or her alone? Join the ranks of single parenthood? You don't have to do any of that. Marry me.''

She clamped a hand over her mouth, pushing his hand away, vaguely aware of his dark expression as she darted from her office and raced for the small bathroom nearby.

He was waiting, leaning against the wall outside the door, when she finally emerged. She'd expected no less, but she hadn't expected to see Maisy standing there with him. Still shaky, Mel strongly considered closing herself back in the bathroom.

"You didn't eat any breakfast this morning, did you," Maisy said, her arms crossed. "You only get sick when you don't eat."

"I'm fine," she assured. She ignored Luke. "Now, I've got to get started on the inventory."

"No. You're going to take the day off and rest."

Mel saw past Maisy's tart tone to her concern. "I don't need the day off. I just need to get back to work." Which she couldn't do as long as they blocked her way.

Maisy's eyes narrowed. "Don't go back to your office today, chicken. Inventory can wait." She looked up at Luke and sniffed. "Be of some use and make sure she does as I say. And here." She stuck a pink message slip into his hand. "Dr. Frame called looking for you. He said to call him back pronto." She strode down the wood-floored hallway, her heels clacking in tempo to the curls vibrating on her head.

"Does she know?" The message slip disappeared into his pocket.

"That I'm pregnant?" She smiled falsely. "It's become hard to disguise."

His jaw tightened. "Does she know that I'm the father?"

Her burst of sarcasm dwindled. She shook her head. "Nobody knows."

He seemed to think about that. "Well, I don't know about you, but I don't have the nerve to ignore her. So, come on."

Mel glared at Luke. "Very funny."

He didn't look particularly humorous. "At least Maisy figures it's your lack of food that had you tossing your cookies in there. Wonder what she'd think if she knew the real reason. Marriage proposals always make you nauseous or is it just mine in particular?''

Her stomach gave a dangerous lurch. ''That wasn't a proposal. That was a demand.'' She brushed past him, heading back to her office. ''I told you before that I wasn't husband hunting.''

She had long legs, but his were longer. He blocked her office doorway. ''Is Maisy right? Have you eaten?''

''Move aside, please.''

''Answer the question.''

''Stop treating me as if I cannot think for myself!''

''I'm only asking if you've eaten. I'm—''

''High-handed.'' And she'd had enough of that to last her a lifetime.

''—concerned.'' His lips were tight. ''That's my baby you're carrying. Have you even had proper care?''

''Dr. Hugo is—''

''Lackadaisical at best.''

Mel caught her breath. ''You are unbelievable. How dare you cast aspersions on Dr. Hugo. He's delivered countless children.''

''The man doesn't even order X rays when he should. And he hasn't delivered any kids of mine.''

''Knock up a lot of women, do you?'' Mel sucked in her breath, wishing the words back.

''Only you, sweetheart. Only you.''

Her heart was racing, her breath short. She felt dizzy suddenly, and saw the shadows in Luke's blue eyes clear as he swore under his breath and caught her about the waist just as her knees gave way.

"Don't." She closed her eyes, willing away the whirling sensation as he swept her up in his arms as if she were no bigger than April.

"Shut up." He turned away from her office, striding down the hall. "Do you have a room here in the inn, or someplace else of your own?"

Her eyes prickled. She did *not* want to cry. "Put me down. Go call Dr. Frame back. If I'm lucky, he's calling your vacation short because they can't manage without you."

He stopped at an intersection of hallways. "I guarantee you that isn't it," he said shortly. "Which way, Mel? Or should I just find Maisy and ask her?" He looked toward the lobby where Maisy's voice could be heard as she spoke to someone.

"You play dirty."

"All's fair in love and war."

"We're not in love," she said sharply.

He looked down at her, his eyes unreadable. "Which way am I going, Mel?"

He needed a shave. His lean cheeks were shadowed, but she could still detect the muscle twitching in his tight jaw. Were they at war, then? She didn't want that any more than she wanted to lose herself in another impossible relationship. A hot tear slipped from the corner of her eye. "I have my own cottage," she whispered.

"Where?"

"Out back. There's a turnoff on the path right before the Blue Cottage." She swiped at her damp cheek. If he said one single thing about their cottages being in such close proximity, she wasn't sure what she'd do.

Kicking him was out of the question considering the way he held her.

His gaze captured hers. For once, there was nothing angry, demanding or patronizing there. Only simple reassurance. "It'll be okay, Mel."

She felt her mulishness fade. The foolish thing was that she wanted to believe him. She swallowed the knot in her throat and blinked back more of the stupid, weak tears that wanted to break free. "Would you put me down, please? Before someone sees us."

"Are you going to run away from me again?"

"I'm hardly in shape to run these days."

He let her legs go slowly to the floor, which left him standing so close to her she could feel the heat off his body. Her swollen abdomen was pressed against him.

The baby kicked.

Hard.

His gaze dropped, looking at that spot, focusing so intently that Mel felt weak from it.

Time shrank down to a limitless pinpoint as his hand lifted. His fingers were long, sturdy and strong looking. Veins defined the back of his hand. It was a thoroughly, utterly masculine hand. One that held a fine tremble as he slowly pressed his palm, fingers widespread, against the swell of her child. His child. *Their* child.

She felt the warmth of his touch through her thin cotton dress. Felt the warmth and that tremor, almost like a vibration, right through her. For an odd moment, she found herself thinking about the tuning fork her music teacher had loved to wave about during the private lessons her parents had insisted upon. Mel still couldn't play the piano or the harp or the violin to save her soul.

But the tuning fork had always fascinated her. Her teacher had given it to her when she finally retired from the job. It was one of the few items Mel had taken with her when she'd walked away from the shambles of her life four years earlier.

In that moment Mel knew what she'd done about Luke had been wrong. All the months of justifying her silence over the matter were for naught.

"I'm sorry." Her voice was husky. "I should have notified you."

She heard him slowly exhale, as if he'd been waiting for that admission for a lifetime. "Yeah." He didn't cut her any slack. "And I should have called."

Her disquiet deepened. "Why? You couldn't have known this happened." On cue, the baby bumped against his hand.

A ghost of a smile played about his lips. "I told you, Mel. I couldn't stop thinking about you."

Before she could defuse that particularly explosive nugget, he ushered her through the rear of the inn, out the open dining area that had now been cleared of food and guests and down the stone steps to the path.

He kept steady hold of her arm as they walked to her cottage. Inside, his gaze traveled over the interior of her cottage. It was almost identical to the Blue Cottage. Except her bedroom was half the size of the one in Luke's cottage; the bed half the size of the ocean-wide thing there.

She lifted her arm out of his hold and moved away

from him as surely as she moved away from thoughts of him and the size of the bed in his cottage.

Her kitchen was little more than a row of cupboards, a small refrigerator and a cooktop against the far wall. Ordinarily Mel would have bristled at the sight of Luke ''entering'' her kitchen area, where he began rummaging around in the cupboard and refrigerator without one word to her.

But she felt so tired that she didn't utter a single protest. She sank down on the oversize chair that had seen her through countless sleepless nights when she'd first come to Turnabout. With fat arms, a deep seat and a thickly pillowed back, the chair almost seemed to wrap around her with comforting familiarity.

She leaned her head back, watching Luke beneath her lowered lids. He was wearing shorts again. Slouchy, baggy things that didn't detract at all from the strength and shape of his long legs. And he moved easily. Confidently. As casually as if he'd rummaged through her cupboards a hundred times before, as if there was nothing more important or momentous on his mind beyond fixing some food.

It was almost possible to convince herself that she'd imagined his marriage proposal. *Almost.*

She prayed he didn't bring it up again. She wasn't sure her nerves could take it.

In minutes, he handed her a plate filled with a fluffy egg concoction, sliced cantaloupe and two slices of toast.

She slowly took the plate. ''You cut the crusts off the toast.''

He turned back to the kitchen. ''Habit.''

Frowning a little, she picked up the perfectly golden toast and took a bite. Her parents' cook had trimmed crusts from the bread. Somehow, it was hard to visualize Luke—dangerous looking with his untamed hair and whisker-roughened cheeks—doing the same task that fussbudget Reeves had performed in the pristine kitchen he'd claimed as his domain.

At least Luke hadn't skimmed a thin coating of marmalade on the toast before presenting it to her. Not that she had marmalade in her cupboards since she hated the stuff. "Habit from what?" *From whom?*

At her question, she sensed more than saw his shoulders stiffen and she realized she'd swum into sensitive waters.

Her gaze shifted from the set of Luke's broad shoulders beneath his loose tan shirt to a small, framed photo sitting on the mosaic-tiled end table beside her chair. Understanding someone else's need for privacy was second nature to her now.

Biting her lip, she drew her fingertip along the frame. Then she quietly slipped the frame into the table's narrow drawer alongside that small tuning fork from her music lesson days before picking up the fork he'd provided. She lifted a bite of the eggs to her mouth.

Demanding, intense and a surgeon, for God's sake. Could she possibly have found a more impossible man to complicate her life?

But oh, he could cook. And she was suddenly ravenous.

Too bad that once she got her shakes out of the way, she was definitely going to make sure he left her alone.

She'd come too far in her life since her arrival on

Turnabout. She'd put the pieces of herself back together in a shape that was far more satisfying than the weak, submissive soul she'd once been as the pretty little trophy of the powerful Dr. Jonathan Deerfield.

No matter *what* Luke said, there was no way that Mel could go back to that kind of life.

No way, at all.

Chapter 8

"How come you are watching me this afternoon instead of Grandma or Lily?"

Mel smiled into April's inquisitive face. "Because Lily had an appointment and your grandma went with her. So I get to stay with you, instead."

Though she'd heard the explanation that day already, April nodded with satisfaction. "This was a good surprise," she decided.

Mel laughed softly. "Yes." She kissed April's nose, then leaned back on her hands, looking at the laden bushes surrounding their grassy picnic spot. "I need daisies," she said. "Which ones are the daisies?"

April rolled her eyes and pointed with uncanny accuracy. "Those ones. How come you don't know your flowers, Mel? Grammy says you're supersmart but I keep having to *teach* you 'bout the flowers."

Mel shrugged, making her eyes wide. A master's in

language studies did not a botanist make. "I guess I'm not as smart as you, kiddo."

April giggled and rolled onto her back as Mel leaned over and plucked a half-dozen stems from the bush next to them. She stared up at the blue sky. "Grammy says my mom's in heaven."

Mel sat back down, automatically weaving the flower stems together. Maisy was convinced that her daughter was dead. For Maisy believed that nothing would have kept Tessa Fielding from returning to her baby. "Yes. I know."

"Do you s'pose she'll like me?"

"Who?"

"My mom. When I go to heaven."

Mel's heart squeezed. How badly she wanted to assure the girl that was something that wouldn't happen anytime soon. "Of course. Everybody likes you, but your mother does most of all."

"I can't remember her."

Mel's fingers fumbled. She picked up the flower she had dropped and fit it into place. "I know."

"I wish I had friends."

Mel frowned. "Of course you have friends, pumpkin."

"Not like the other kids do. They get to spend the night at each other's houses, and go to parties—"

"Your grandmother threw you a huge party for your birthday."

April's narrow shoulders moved. "I know. It was fun." She blew out a little breath. "I just wish Grammy would let me spend the night at Lani's." Lani was Lily's little sister and the friend closest to April's age.

"Have you asked her?"

April nodded. "She's afraid to let me go, though. In case o' something happening." She turned her head and peered at Mel through eyes as wise as time. "I think it'll be soon. You know. Grammy doesn't want me to say that. It upsets her. She thinks I don't understand what all the doctors told her."

Her throat felt tight. "I know, baby."

"I do understand, though. And Grammy will be all alone when I go. Except for you and Lily and Dr. Hugo."

"And Tomas and Leo and everybody else on this island who loves your grandmother," Mel assured gently.

"And your baby when he's born. Grammy says she doesn't want you to do the same thing my mom did."

Mel's fingers paused over the flowers. "Oh?"

"She went off the island when I was a baby to look for my dad, but she never came back."

Mel didn't see how her situation could at all be compared to that of Maisy's daughter, who'd desperately loved the man with whom she'd conceived her child. Definitely not the same as Mel's case at all.

She handed April the daisies she'd woven together into a wreath. "There you go."

Older than her years, April was nevertheless still a delighted child. She sat up and plopped the wreath on her blond curls, her face breaking into a grin as her fingers nimbly felt out the details of the flowers atop her curls. "I'm a marrying girl, now!"

Mel couldn't help but smile at the child's glee, even

though she wanted to rail at the hand April had been dealt.

April pushed to her feet, her arms held out wide. She slowly twirled, then stopped and took the wreath from her own head to drop it unerringly on Mel's. "Did Dr. Luke put the baby in you?"

Standing on the path, not ten feet from the patch of grass surrounded by gloriously blooming plants, Luke heard the piping of the child's question.

Eavesdroppers never hear good of themselves. The remembered words of his grandfather swam in Luke's head. He'd had a sleepless night followed by a restless morning. So restless that he'd gone to see Hugo, if only to keep his mind occupied on anything other than the twists life had thrown him. He stopped cold on the opposite side of the bushes, and waited.

He could see the top of Mel's gilded head. Could see, too, the child that Jason had wanted him to evaluate the first time he'd come to Turnabout. It was the closest he'd ever been to April.

And she was looking straight at him with the most vivid green eyes he'd ever seen. He knew from Hugo that her vision was seriously deteriorating because of the tumor. But he would have sworn in that moment that she was looking right into his eyes, seeing everything—good and bad and worse—that was hidden there.

"Did he, Mel?" the child prompted.

"Where did you get that idea, April?"

"From Grammy."

Luke had the strangest sense that April's gaze was filled with sympathy as she eyed him over the bushes.

Which was impossible on so many levels it was laughable. She was only curious about the suspicion her grandmother must have voiced. And sympathy? He was probably only a sizable blob of shadow in her vision.

"Yes." Mel's voice was soft. Even. Giving little clue to the child what her feelings were on that reality. Still Luke felt tension leak out of him as surely as a spent balloon when Mel freely admitted the truth.

April's head tilted and her curls danced in the faint breeze, reminding him uncannily of her grandmother. "Is it fun to be in love?"

"I...beg your pardon?"

"Grammy says that's how you get a baby. By loving someone. But Dr. Hugo loves Grandma and she doesn't have a baby. She won't even kiss him 'cause of the curse."

Luke raised his eyebrows. *Hugo and Maisy? Curse?*

Mel suddenly turned, her eyes widening with shock at the sight of him across the blossoms. "How long have you been standing there?"

Luke stepped through one of the breaks in the row of plants. She started to get up and he touched her shoulder, staying her. "Not long."

He looked at the little girl. She was petite, appeared to be underweight, with translucent skin as pale as snow. "You must be April. I've heard a lot about you. I'm Luke."

The girl preened and, despite her delicacy, her smile was wide and thoroughly engaging, full of spirit and life. Luke's stomach felt hollow. Damn Jason and his bloody interfering ways! Had he known all along that one look at the girl would be enough to fell Luke at the knees?

Of course he had. Jason was no fool. That was probably the reason for the phone message Luke still hadn't returned. Jason probably wanted to reel them all in, satisfied that he was solving two problems in one. Getting April the help she needed, and getting Luke back in a saddle he wasn't certain fit him anymore.

Then Luke felt small fingers close around his hand and April was tugging him down to the red-and-white-checkered cloth spread across the grass. "You sit next to Mel," she ordered. "You can have my sandwich and we'll all have a picnic together."

From the corner of his eye, Luke watched Mel, waited for her protest. "I think *you* should eat your sandwich, April," was all she said.

April wrinkled her nose. "I don't want it. My head hurts today. But Luke can have it!" With hardly a fumble, she rummaged in the basket beside her and pulled out a wrapped sandwich that she stuck out for him to take.

Mel nibbled the inside of her lip, watching Luke. He'd shaved and his dark hair was pulled back in a leather thong. Why it didn't make him look less dangerous, she didn't know. His jaw was a sharp blade, his lips tightly held. As he reached over and took the offered sandwich from April, she saw the muscle twitching in his jaw.

But his voice was that same, kind tone it had been the night on the beach, as he thanked April for the sandwich and unwrapped it when April told him to do so.

When he took a bite of the peanut butter, tuna and banana concoction that April loved, and even managed to smile and swallow it, Mel felt something inside her soften.

She stared down at her own sandwich. A thankfully ordinary peanut butter and honey mixture. The baby kicked. She looked up and realized Luke was watching her. He'd taken another bite.

Her eyes burned. Why did he have to be *kind?* She could withstand most anything except that.

"Eat your sandwich, Mel," April ordered, sounding so much like Maisy that she couldn't help smiling again. Judging by Luke's expression, he'd thought the same thing.

Feeling that odd disquiet again, Mel silently consumed the sandwich. She knew that April's spurt of energy would soon wane. On other afternoons they'd spent together, the girl would take a nap, after which they'd walk back to Maisy's cottage. But that afternoon, instead of curling up next to Mel on the checkered cloth, the child plopped down on Luke's lap and slipped her fingers through his, giggling a little over the way his dwarfed hers.

Mel saw him close his eyes for a moment, his face suddenly pale. She was on her knees, automatically reaching out to touch his arm, when he looked at her. His expression was so harsh, so darkly wounded, that she froze in place.

Beneath his chin, April hummed off-key as she played with his long fingers. Around them was the heady scent of lavender, daisies, gardenia, all carried on the gentle, constant breeze.

And Luke looked at her with a world of pain in his eyes that she recognized only too well.

Grief. Guilt. Despair.

Her heart ached. Her fingers stretched toward his arm, almost grazing his bronzed skin.

Then he blinked, and it was as if Mel had never seen a single thing out of the ordinary in his sapphire eyes.

Feeling off balance, she sat back, her hand slowly falling to her side.

Eventually April dozed off. And still they sat there on the patch of grass. Silent. Luke looking lost in his thoughts. Mel wondering who this man was who'd eat an inedible sandwich in order to please a child whose presence seemed to cause him pain.

The baby kicked again and she shifted, absently trying to find a comfortable position. She finally lay back, flat, keeping her knees bent. A vision of a beached whale hovered on the edge of her thoughts.

"What curse was April talking about?"

"How long were you standing there eavesdropping?" One glance at him told her he wouldn't be answering that question. "Turns believe it is bad luck to fall in love with an outsider." It was the short explanation.

"What makes them believe that?"

"Because tragedy always follows." She looked at April sleeping in his arms. The beautiful child was a result of one such union that had ended in disaster. "There's a hundred-year-old curse that promises it. But don't ask me the origin of the curse, because as long as I've lived here, nobody has ever told me. Being an outsider, and all."

"Do you believe the curse yourself?"

"I'm not a Turn."

"Where *are* you from?"

"Is this *Twenty Questions?*"

"Are you hiding out here, Mel?"

"Yes. From the Feds. I'm wanted in twenty states." She made a face. "Born and raised most properly in Northern California and not hiding in the least." At least not from anything but her own emotions.

She bent her arm over her eyes, shading them from the sun. "What about you? Have you always been in Arizona?" She asked only out of politeness, she assured herself, not because there was an insatiable curiosity burning inside her.

"No. She's had surgery already, hasn't she."

Mel sighed faintly. She turned her head to find Luke watching her. April was sound asleep in his arms, so trusting that it broke Mel's heart a little. *I'm sorry, Maisy.* "Yes."

His fingers smoothed over the girl's head. "There was recurrence."

"Yes."

"Jason didn't know about the previous surgery."

"Maisy doesn't talk about it much. Certainly not with her guests, even if they are regulars. Maisy doesn't trust outsiders easily and she's very protective when it comes to April."

"I noticed." His voice was dry as dust. "Yet she trusts you. An outsider."

"She's my boss and my friend." The urge to make him understand Maisy was swift and compelling, if confusing. She'd never before felt a need to defend

Maisy to anyone. "She came to this island as a girl and later married a local man. He died shortly after their only child—April's mother—was born. Nearly everyone she's loved has been lost because of someone or something from off-island. Her husband. Her daughter."

"Proving the curse, I suppose."

"You don't have to believe it, Luke. The point is that Maisy does. There was a, um, a surgeon who heard about April's condition when she was a toddler. He convinced Maisy that he could help. So Maisy took April off Turnabout for treatment. It was two years of misery. And still the tumor returned less than twelve months later. So there was another battery of exams, consultants, therapies. Nothing changed. Even the original surgeon had to admit defeat. There just aren't cases like hers. Maisy refuses to put April through more than she's already had to endure. She wants her to have some enjoyment in her young life."

"Who was the surgeon?"

Mel frowned. "Why?"

He smoothed his hand through April's curls. They sprang back, coiled around his fingers. "Maybe I know of him."

Mel swallowed. Why had she gotten into this? "Deerfield. Something like that." She rolled onto her side and began pushing herself to her feet. "Would you mind staying here with her?"

"What's wrong?"

"Nothing. Just—" her cheeks felt warm "—you know. Nothing."

"Too much water in too little space," he deduced,

his lips twitching. "Why don't I carry April, and you ladies can finish the afternoon out of the sun. You're starting to get sunburned."

Before she could protest, he'd risen with nary a jiggle to disturb April, who slept on.

Since it *was* hot and bright, Mel didn't feel compelled to argue the point. She also didn't want to continue wading in the conversation that she'd gotten involved in through nobody's fault but her own. She quickly shook out the cloth and folded it inside the picnic basket, gathered up April's collection of toys and slipped through the bushes to the path that led back to the cottages.

She knew that Maisy and Lily would be some time, yet. But she also knew that Maisy's cottage was unlocked, so she led the way there. It was a little closer than her own, and April could finish her nap in her own bed.

Her urgency lending a little speed to her steps, they made short work of the walk and, leaving Luke to take care of April, Mel hastily visited the bathroom. When she came out, the faint hope that he might have gone on his way was quickly dashed, for he sat on the rattan love seat in Maisy's living room, looking very much like a man who'd come to stay.

"There's some ice water for you," he said when he saw her. And sure enough, two glasses were sitting on the coffee table right there among Maisy's magazines and April's fat crayons.

"What? No milk?" Mel regretted the peevish question as soon as it emerged.

"Buttermilk," he said. "Somehow I didn't figure you'd welcome that."

She shuddered. The truth was, she didn't like drinking any kind of milk. She'd already choked down her daily quota of the stuff, and unless it came in the welcome form of a thick chocolate milkshake, she was free from milk for another day. "No."

There was a pile of clean, folded towels on the chair, leaving Mel no place to sit but beside him. She picked up the glass of water. Put it back down.

"I've met Deerfield. At a symposium," Luke said. "Brilliant surgeon. If it was John Deerfield, that is. Folks called him 'the great knife.'"

Mel shot to her feet.

"You okay?"

She nodded. "Yes. Of course. My, um, my back hurts some. I'm more comfortable moving around." Her hand rubbed absently over the hard thump the baby gave her at the lie. She looked out the window at the ocean view. "Is the Blue Cottage still comfortable for you?"

"It was, last I checked." His voice was dry. "I'm not going to shackle you off to the preacher, Mel, so relax."

"I don't know why you said that in the first place." It was proof that her hormones were wreaking havoc with her common sense, for why should she feel irked that he so easily backed off his marriage demand-proposal when she didn't want to marry him or anyone else, anyway?

"Because I want my child to know I exist."

"Marriage is no guarantee of that. I know people

who've been married decades who don't know their children.''

"Is that why you haven't talked to your parents in four years? Because they didn't understand you?"

Mel lifted one shoulder. Admitting the truth seemed easier than trying to come up with some other plausible excuse. "What I wanted from my life and what they wanted for my life were two very different things." They'd been horrified, for one thing, when she walked away from her hollow marriage.

"At least they cared enough to *have* something in mind that they wanted for you."

She turned from the ocean view. "Your parents didn't?"

His lips twisted. "Not even close. My grandfather raised us."

"Us?"

"My sister and me."

"I always wanted a brother or a sister. Where is she now? Your sister. Does she live in Arizona, too?"

"She died when she was fourteen."

Sympathy settled inside her. "I'm sorry."

"So am I." He looked at his hands. "It's the reason I decided to go to med school. She shouldn't have died. I've done countless procedures for neurological conditions exactly like hers. Successfully." He flexed his fingers once then closed them in fists that belied the calm expression on his face. "Her doctors gave up on her too soon. Just like April."

Mel flinched. "Luke, you don't know what it's been like for them." She started toward him, but a crippling pain in her leg stopped her cold.

Luke was on his feet like a shot when she involuntarily cried out. "What is it?"

Feeling stupid, she couldn't help wincing again. "Charley horse," she muttered. "I keep getting them in my—oh!—leg."

She heard him exhale. "Damn, woman, you about gave me a heart attack, you know that?" Without waiting for a response, he swept her over to the love seat, settling her on one end, him on the other, facing her. "You probably need more calcium," he said. His hand was gentle as he lifted her leg in his hands.

He slid off her sandal, tossed it onto the floor and brushed the long folds of her dress aside. Then his palms circled her ankle and slid up over the knot in her cramping calf. "There?"

Mel swallowed, words strangling in her throat. "It's fine, Luke, really."

"Right." He was looking at her leg as if he could see through to the knotted muscle. His hands were warm, his fingers gentle. He slid one hand behind her knee, lifting a little as he kneaded with the other hand. "Relax," he said quietly. "I can make it better."

"That sounds a little too close to 'trust me, little girl, this won't hurt.'" She jerked when his touch honed in with painful accuracy.

That same ghost of a smile haunted his lips. "Don't you trust me?"

A tart retort died on her lips, to be replaced by painful honesty. "It's not necessarily you I don't trust."

Chapter 9

Mel's words hung in the air. Luke kept working on her muscle spasm and tried not to notice how smooth and supple her skin felt beneath his fingers.

"What's not to trust?" He asked the question even though he wasn't sure it would be good to hear the answer. Particularly when he had his hands on her naked leg and his curiosity about what she might or might not have on underneath the airy dress was heading right off the scale.

She shifted, winced a little. "Luke…" Then she didn't say anything more. She just looked at him, with eyes that were so wide and so brown.

His touch slowed. Became less therapeutic and a lot more tactile. He was too damned old to have his hormones jumping through hoops the way they were. But he was hanged if he could make himself take his hands off her sweet, smooth leg.

Beneath her knee, his fingers drifted back and forth, and he felt a fine shiver work through her. Saw the way her hands moved just slightly, the way her head lifted infinitesimally, her lips drawing in, then softening as she exhaled a soft whisper of sound that raised every nerve in his body.

"Stop," she whispered.

"Charley horse gone?"

"You know it is."

So why didn't he stop touching her? Why did he keep running his hand over her calf? Curving up over her knee, grazing the velvety skin of her taut thigh.

Folds of yellow fabric pooled against her thighs. How many times had he used the memory of their shared time to get him through another nightmare-studded night? And on those rare occasions when he hadn't been plagued by the nightmare, he had awakened in the morning, aching for the feel of her silky hair slipping through his fingers, the press of her soft lips against his.

He ran his hands all the way up her thighs, only some deeply ingrained common sense making him keep to the outside of her dress, and he curved his hands up over the firm jut of her belly. "It wasn't just sex," he muttered. Then he lowered his head, pressing his mouth against the swell of their child.

She sucked in her breath, her hands closing over his shoulders, sinking into his hair. He expected her to protest, to pull at his head, but she did none of those things. She trembled wildly and smoothed her hand over his hair down to the band he'd restrained it in.

"Don't do this to me." Her voice was low, shaking.

"It's too easy. Too easy to lose myself. I can't do that again."

"Nobody has to lose anything." He braced one hand against the back of the love seat and the other on the edge beneath the cushion under them, and levered himself up, keeping his weight off her. He brushed his mouth over hers. "Our baby won't be losing anything. Marry me."

She pushed against his chest so abruptly that he nearly fell off the small sofa. He caught himself and ended up on the coffee table where the glasses of ice water promptly tipped over, dousing him but good.

He swore under his breath and jumped up.

She clapped her hands over her mouth. Luke had the momentary thought that she was going to be sick again, but then her shoulders shook and he heard her laughter.

His shorts were soaked. Maybe it was a good thing. He heard himself laugh, too. It felt a little rusty, but it was a laugh.

And it felt good.

"You look like you had too much water in too little space." Mel's eyes danced. "That'll teach you to mess with a pregnant lady."

That's all it took for Luke to go from ice-water cold right back to hot. Still smiling, he studied her lips longer than was wise or polite. Long enough for her to know exactly where his thoughts had returned.

"Don't look at me that way."

"What way?"

She swallowed, hard. He saw it in the movement of her long, lovely neck. She moistened her lips. "Like, like—"

''I want to make love to you right here, right now?''
Her nipples were rigid, pushing impudently against the
modest lines of her yellow dress. She was ripe with his
child and he'd never been more aroused in his life.

She swallowed again, groaning a little. ''Luke—''

''But we won't. Not here. Not now.'' It was Maisy's
cottage, after all, and the child napping in the other
room could awaken at any time.

Desire swept through Mel like wildfire, dizzying her
with it. But it didn't matter. Because further involvement with Luke Trahern was out of the question.
''Not...ever.'' Oh, why was it so hard to push that
word past her lips? And why did he have to just stand
there, his hands propped on his hips, his eyes too wise,
too knowing, looking dark and dangerous and like
every good little girl's fantasy come to life? ''I m-mean
it, Luke. Not ever. We're not going to do that. Once
was quite enough. Obviously.''

''It was twice,'' he reminded softly. ''And who are
you trying to convince with your protests? Agree to
marry me or don't agree, yet. I'm not going to stop
pushing for what I know is right, so you might as well
get used to it. Regardless, you and I are going to end
up in bed together, Mel. It's a matter of time, and you
know it.''

Then she could only sit there, speechless, when he
leaned down. Her hands clutched at the cushion under
her, but the onslaught of his mouth on hers never came.
He looked at her, then pressed a soft kiss to her forehead, ran his finger down her cheek and left.

Well after the click of the screen door sounded, Mel
finally remembered to breathe. She let out her air in a

whoosh, and just sat there, her heart thundering as his
words circled in her mind and his baby kicked in her
womb.

Mel didn't see Luke again that day. April eventually
woke from her nap, but she had such a violent head-
ache that Mel gave her a dose of her medication and
she went right back to sleep. Maisy returned, took one
look at the prescription bottle that Mel had left on the
coffee table and paled.

Mel fixed her friend some tea and a sandwich and
quietly left. She'd learned long ago that there were
times when Maisy was up for company, and times
when she wasn't.

Tomas handled most of the duties on the weekend,
and Mel usually caught up on her own laundry and
personal matters during that time. But once she had
hurried to her cottage, half afraid she'd see Luke on
the way and half afraid she wouldn't, she couldn't
seem to concentrate on even the most mundane tasks.
When night fell with no sign of Luke, she convinced
herself she was grateful.

The next morning, after an impossibly restless night,
she was doubly convinced that his absence was for the
best. Maybe he'd reconsidered his crazy words, his impossible proposal.

By the time that afternoon rolled around, Mel felt as
if she were going crazy herself. Her laundry was still
undone, her small refrigerator still unstocked. Rattling
around her cottage with Luke's only a few dozen steps
away was making her nuts and she finally took refuge

in her office at the inn. But even there she felt disjointed.

It was proof of her own madness when she found herself holding the phone in her hand, dialing her parents' number. It was further proof of her cowardice when, at the sound of Reeves's ponderous voice answering the phone, she quickly pressed her finger over the disconnect button.

"I thought you didn't work on Sundays."

She sat back in her chair, so startled by the voice at her doorway that she fumbled and the phone clattered noisily as she replaced the receiver. "Luke."

"Well?" He leaned his shoulder against the doorjamb. "It's Sunday. What are you doing here in the office?"

Trying to pretend none of this—you, me, the baby— is happening. She didn't voice the thought. "Playing catch-up." It wasn't quite a lie. She did have some paperwork to take care of.

He lifted one eyebrow and she had the insane thought that maybe he'd read her mind. Which was nonsense, of course. "Important stuff?" he asked.

"Very." Seeing as how it had waited two weeks and could easily wait two more. "Where have you been, anyway?" She wanted to kick herself for voicing the question.

"I was talking to Hugo."

"The man you think is incompetent."

"I never said that."

"No. *Lackadaisical* was your word of choice, as I recall."

"Well, he was right about Leo's ankle, as it happens. There was no fracture."

For a moment she was surprised that he'd so easily admit it. "How do you know that?"

"I found out where Leo lived and went there myself."

"Double-checking Hugo's work."

"Am I supposed to apologize?"

"Maybe to Dr. Hugo."

"Maybe I did," he said evenly.

She wasn't certain if he was serious, or not. In her personal experience, apologies weren't in a surgeon's vocabulary. But more than once, now, Luke had offered one when due. "Why does any of this matter to you, anyway? Turnabout needs one doctor, but it doesn't have a large enough population to support two."

He watched her. "Afraid I'm looking to relocate here, Mel?"

Her stomach dropped. "You're a pediatric neurosurgeon."

"Who'd likely only have one patient on the island— a girl whose grandmother won't let her be examined."

"I told you all that they'd been through—"

He shook his head, cutting her off. "So you did." He came into her office and sat on the corner of her desk, bringing with him the warmth of the day, the scent of the ocean. "I've spent some time with Hugo lately. Maybe I'm considering a switch to general practice."

Her jaw loosened as she actually considered the statement as truth. It took only a moment, however, for the ridiculousness of it to penetrate. "No, you're not. You'd be bored stiff inside a week. People go into surgical specialties for the demand of it, the adrenal high, the power. You'd never find that in general—" His eyebrow had risen again and she realized her mouth was seriously running away with her.

"And you consider yourself an expert on that because...why?" He waited.

His attitude smacked of superiority. She'd left behind that sort of attitude from her father, from Jonathan, but she still saw red. "Because I was born and raised by Daddy the surgeon, and his good little wife," she snapped. "Now, would you please go?" She lifted several reservation forms and shook them. "I have work to do."

"I never was good at listening to orders," he said mildly. "So, your dad was a surgeon. Does he still practice?"

She wished she'd kept her mouth shut. She'd never had trouble with that before. What *was* it about this man that got under her nerves so thoroughly? "He... teaches."

"No kidding?" He inexorably tugged the forms from her and set them aside, but he didn't release her hand. His thumb smoothed over the backs of her knuckles, setting all manner of sensation skittering through her. "Where?"

"At a university." Where he was dean of the college of medicine.

"Full of more details, Mel?"

She couldn't think straight when he touched her. That *had* to be the answer. He touched her, and her brain short-circuited. What other explanation could there be? "Please let go of my hand."

A whisper of a smile entered his eyes. "Something wrong?" He placed her hand between both of his, looking at her palm, smoothing his fingers slowly over it in a manner reminiscent of the palm readers who'd set up shop on Fisherman's Wharf, catering to the tourists.

"Luke, really, I have work to do." It was a blatant lie, but she was getting desperate.

"I'll let you go for a price."

Her lips parted. "I *beg* your pardon?"

The smile spread to his lips. "Where is your mind at, Melanie? Mel is short for Melanie, isn't it?"

She nodded, feeling flushed. "I prefer Mel."

"What's wrong with your full name?"

It belongs to the woman I used to be. "Too...frilly." She expected him to be amused, and he was.

He turned her hand over, looking at her short, unpolished nails. "You don't have to be wearing ruffles and have paint on your face to be thoroughly female." His gaze met hers. "Believe me, you are *thoroughly* feminine. And Mel suits you."

Her thoroughly feminine hormones were shifting into overdrive. "All right, so let go of my hand now."

He tsked softly. "Impatient, Mel. I might think you're a little unnerved, here."

"Well why not? You're the one who goes around promising bed bouncing."

"Promising?"

"Threatening."

His smile widened. But he did let go of her hand. "Don't you want to know the price?"

"My hand is free." She wiggled her fingers.

In a smooth movement that abruptly reminded her just how quickly the man could move when he felt like it, he'd rolled her chair out and was leaning over her, his hands on either side of her shoulders, effectively trapping her. Her heart skittered and her bravado breathed its last.

"The price is answering one question."

His lips were only inches from hers. She caught herself, barely, from tilting her head, closing the gap. "What?"

"When's your next appointment with Hugo?"

It was the last thing she'd expected. "In a few days."

"Good." He straightened, giving her space to pretend she wasn't reeling from the kiss that *hadn't* come. "I'll go with you."

"I don't—"

"Do you really want to argue with me about this? The baby is mine, too."

And she'd already kept him "out of the loop" long enough. He didn't have to voice the thought; her twanging conscience heard it all the same. Which didn't mean it was all that easy to swallow her objections, even knowing they were unreasonable. "Don't you have to go back to Arizona soon? You can't stay on Turnabout indefinitely." She'd already checked the schedule, but the Blue Cottage still reflected Maisy's supposed renovations and not Luke's presence at all.

"Didn't Dr. Frame call to summon you back? You must have patients."

"You think my going home will get me out of your hair?"

"I can hope."

He laughed softly, but his eyes were dark, serious. "Sorry to disappoint you, honey, but Jase most definitely does not need me. You've got *all* my attention."

For Mel, who'd spent her entire life wishing fruitlessly for the attention of the men she'd loved, his words ought to have been a dream come true.

Somehow, coming from Luke, they felt more like a threat to the semblance of contentment she'd finally managed to obtain. If she lost herself in a relationship with *him,* she wasn't sure she could ever recover.

Chapter 10

"So, you're the mystery father after all."

Mel flushed as Dr. Hugo eyed Luke speculatively.

"Maisy was right, then," he continued. "At least you're both from off-island, so we don't have to worry about the curse. What do you intend to do about our Mel, here?"

"Dr. Hugo!" Mel wanted to sink through the floor of the examining room. "I hardly think that's any—"

"Marry her, only she won't have me. Little does she know just how smart she might be."

Beneath the thin cotton smock with the pale blue flowers that Dr. Hugo's sometime nurse had provided her for the exam, Mel's shoulders stiffened. "Stop talking about me as if I'm not here."

Luke's hand closed over the back of her neck and she caught the seriousness underlying the amusement in his gaze. Her annoyance stuttered. "Can we just get on with this? I've got things to do."

"Haven't you learned anything since you came to Turnabout, Mel?" Hugo washed his hands and pulled out his stethoscope. "Time has a different meaning here. Priorities aren't the same as they are on the mainland."

"Well, if time is different, maybe that's why I'm getting *huge*." Mel was determined to ignore Luke, standing beside her where she sat on the examining table.

"Good thing you showed early," Hugo muttered, "considering how long it took you to finally admit that you were pregnant and not just suffering some flu bug you couldn't shake."

Mel flushed, feeling Luke's quick look at that.

Obviously seeing no reason for discretion, Hugo looked at Luke. "She was nearly four months gone before she came to me, but anybody with a lick of sense could *see* she was expecting."

"I took vitamins before I came to you," Mel said defensively. "Ate right, did everything a person is supposed to do."

"Good thing," Hugo grunted. He listened to her heart, checked her blood pressure, made some notes on his chart, eyed his cigar on the counter but managed to refrain. "Fortunately, you're healthy as a horse, so the baby didn't seem to take any harm from his mama's refusal to see the light of day. All right, let's see how things are going."

"His?"

Hugo grinned. "Manner of speaking, Luke. Don't go getting excited that you're gonna have a son."

"A girl as beautiful as Mel would do just fine."

Mel closed her eyes against Luke's quiet words. "Can we get on with this, please?"

"Only people who make worse patients than doctors themselves are children of doctors." Hugo shook his head. "I oughta know. My daughter won't go near a white coat." He brushed aside the gown, discreetly revealing the bulge of Mel's abdomen. He squirted gel over it then pressed the Doppler against her through the gel, listening closely to the watery rush of sound that came through the amplified device.

Mel saw him frown in the same moment that Luke did. Unease sliced through her way too easily. Without thought, she reached for Luke's hand. "What? What's wrong?"

Hugo waved her silent. He turned and rummaged through his cabinet of tricks and came out with another stethoscope. "Wish we had an ultrasound," he muttered as he pressed the instrument to Mel's belly, his head close as he listened. "I'll be damned," he muttered.

Mel struggled to sit up. "What is it? I can't lose—"

"Twins." Dr. Hugo looked up, grinning. "I'd bet my favorite humidor you've got twins kicking around in there."

All the anxiety racing inside her screeched to a screaming halt. She could hear her heartbeat thumping in her ears. "I...what?"

"Twins, Mel." Luke looked stunned. "Do they run in your family?"

She blinked and shook her head. Turned from Luke to Dr. Hugo. "How can this be?"

Dr. Hugo pulled her gown over her belly and dumped his equipment on the counter behind him. "Well, now, see there's this thing called an egg. Sometimes two. Meets up with sp—"

"Very funny." Mel huffed and fell back against the inclined table.

"Hey," Luke murmured. "Look at it this way." He was still holding her hand, and he kissed her knuckles, looking as pleased as if they'd been planning to have children together for years. "Double the fun."

Mel folded her arm across her eyes. Tears burned behind her eyelids. Two babies. Dear Lord, she could barely face one baby for fear of the past repeating itself. Now there were two? She swallowed. "Maybe you're mistaken. Maybe—"

"Possibly," Dr. Hugo agreed. "If you want to know for certain, you'll have to go off-island. Have an ultrasound. Although they've been fooled by twins now and then, you're far enough along now to get a good looksee at what's happening in there. I can refer you to an OB in San Diego. You two better hold off on, uh, having relations for a while. Least until we have a better picture of your progress."

Mel refused to look at Luke. Relations? That would only happen if they *had* a relationship. Which they most certainly did not.

"I'll make arrangements for the trip immediately," Luke said.

"No. I don't want to go anywhere." She ignored Luke's immediate protest and focused on Dr. Hugo.

"There's no real need for an ultrasound, is there? Twins explains the fact that I'm a little bigger than normal. All my other tests have come back with good results, my blood pressure is within normal—"

"Relax, Mel," Luke said. "Ultrasound is perfectly routine."

She knew that. How well she knew that. "If I had wanted one," she told him, wanting to tear out her hair in the face of his perfectly smooth bedside-manner voice. Jonathan had used that type of voice too many times on her to count, and she still hated it. "I am perfectly capable of having it arranged."

Silence filled the tiny exam room, finally broken by Dr. Hugo, who told her she could get dressed again, and left them alone quite without his usual, characteristically colorful comments.

Mel turned her back on Luke, swinging her legs down from the table, and reached for her dress.

Luke's hand was there first, handing it to her.

"You can forget trying to dress me, too. I'm not entirely inept." She snatched the dress from him and stepped behind the screen in the corner of the room.

"Nobody said you were. And I wouldn't mind dressing you, but first I'd rather *un*dress you." His voice was smooth. "Seeing how we never really got to that part. It was too cold that night on the beach."

Mel closed her eyes, telling herself that the idea held no appeal, that her hormones weren't leapfrogging all over themselves at the mere thought of Luke and the presence or lack of her clothing.

She was almost getting used to lying to herself.

"Very funny." Dressed, she stuffed the gown in the

basket left there for used ones, and stepped from behind the screen.

"Do I look like I'm joking?"

She decided against answering. It just seemed wiser. She picked up her wallet, wrote out a check for Dr. Hugo and left it sitting on the counter where he'd be sure to see it. "I need to get back to Maisy's Place."

She saw him look at the check. "I need to add you to my health insurance," he murmured.

Mel headed for the door. "I'm capable of paying my own bills."

"I didn't say you weren't. But the bills relate to my baby—babies."

"Are you coming, or not?"

He left the check where it lay. "I'm the one who rented the Jeep that we drove here, remember?"

"If you weren't coming, I'd just walk."

"You take this independence thing a step too far, you know."

"Well, maybe it's about time," she said, feeling near tears all over again and not really knowing why.

Maybe it was the result of having her life turned topsy-turvy *twice*...in the form of twins. Twins!

She stopped next to the Jeep. Despite her bravado, she didn't feel up to the task of walking all the way back to the inn.

He opened her door and helped her up. "You know, Mel, you're going to have to deal with what's going on."

"Who says I'm not?"

He snorted softly. "Anybody with two eyes in their head." He rounded the Jeep and climbed behind the wheel. He started the engine and drove out from behind Dr. Hugo's rainbow-hued building. They passed the fields, vibrant with blooms of every shade. He slowed to let a trio of children cross the road, which they did, smiling gap-toothed grins, the kites they held rippling as they ran. Then he was driving again, heading over the highest point of the road, where a person could see all the way to Catalina and beyond if the weather was clear.

She wondered if Luke had really meant it when he'd said she was the only woman to carry his child. Found herself wondering how old he was, if he'd been married, if he had family other than the sister he'd lost. And if he did, why he'd felt that he'd had nowhere else to go when he'd returned to Turnabout.

Thinking about any and all of them was easier than contemplating the news Dr. Hugo had delivered.

"How early did you know?"

She closed her eyes against the incredibly beautiful view. "Pretty early." The honesty was nearly as painful as remembering the unadulterated shock, panic, that she'd lived with during those early days when she'd suspected the impossible had occurred.

"Earlier than four months."

She swallowed. Nodded.

"You told me pregnancy wasn't possible."

"Obviously I was wrong."

He turned the wheel, veering off the road, spewing gravel as they rocked to a halt near the guardrail. "Could you turn off the sarcasm for twenty seconds?"

"No." She fumbled with the door latch.

He caught her arm before she could escape. "Dammit, Mel, what is your problem? If you didn't want the baby—*babies*—so much, you could have done something about it months ago."

Nausea accosted her. "Stop. Please, Luke, I can't... just...stop."

His eyes, so dark they looked nearly black, searched her face. "I can't stop, Mel. Those are *my* children you're carrying. We made them together. Maybe you don't want them, hell, I don't know what's—"

"I *do* want them! That's why I couldn't see Dr. Hugo too early!" She yanked free and pushed out of the vehicle, sliding awkwardly from the seat.

Luke was taller and moved a lot faster. He was around the Jeep in a flash, catching up to her before she made it to the guardrail overlooking the cliff. He grabbed her wrists, making her face him. "Every time you walk away, I'm going to be right behind you."

She cast him a look that could have broken the heart of a granite statue. He gentled his grip, moving his hands from shackling her wrists to cupping her shoulders. He could feel her trembling. Without another thought, he pulled her into his arms, shushing her protest, holding her close, cushioning the unnamed emotion that racked her.

Maybe it wasn't the wisest course. Following his instincts lately had mostly been disastrous. But after a long while, after he'd held her, smoothed his hand over her slender back, brushed his hand again and again down her thick, silky hair, he felt her shift.

Then he felt her arms sliding around his waist, fingers clutching the back of his shirt. A long shudder rippled through her. Between them, the babies bumped.

He pressed his cheek to the top of her head, breathing in the clean scent of her hair, feeling the wash of an ocean breeze drift over, coil around them.

The tension seemed to slowly fade, and as it did, the utter silence of the island seemed to penetrate Luke's senses.

His life had changed on this island. Regardless of the circumstances, he was going to be a father. And there wasn't a cell in him that didn't want to howl at the moon in satisfaction. He wanted the babies.

He wanted Mel.

And for some reason, this woman was afraid of being pregnant, afraid of having a baby, afraid of being involved.

He slid his fingers through her hair again, finding the action as soothing to him as it might be to her. "I know pregnancy is scary, Mel—" He felt her start to stiffen up all over again, but held her snug against him, willing her to stay calm. If ever there was a person who cried out for connection with another human being, it was this prickly, intensely private woman. "Particularly the first time around, but I'm going to be with you every step of the way. You're not in this alone."

She pressed her forehead to his shoulder. "This isn't my first pregnancy." Her voice was muffled.

Luke's hand hesitated as he made another pass through the hair lying across her shoulders. A dozen questions, theories, flew through his thoughts, but he voiced none of them. The fact that she did not have a child with her on Turnabout spoke volumes. "It's my first," he said.

She laughed brokenly, then slid her arm around his neck. "I wondered if you'd meant that."

"I did."

Her fingers tightened, her face turning against his neck. "I'm scared, Luke."

Her voice was barely audible, and the admission rocked him. He'd known she was frightened; he hadn't exaggerated when he'd made that comment about anyone being able to see that. Mel's emotions showed so clearly on her beautiful face. But to hear her admit it, the words raw on her voice, made something inside him ache. "Of what?"

Her shoulders moved. He felt her soft breath on his jaw. "Everything."

God, he couldn't take it. Knowing she was scared, hurting, and there wasn't a damned thing he could do about it—particularly when she wouldn't tell him any reason why. "It'll be okay," he murmured, thinking they were some of the most useless words in the English vocabulary.

She looked up at him, her eyes even darker against her pale skin. "You don't know that. Nobody ever knows that."

"Then you've gotta have faith."

"Faith didn't work before."

He absorbed that. "Then have faith in me," he said. "Have faith in this." He covered her mouth with his.

He felt the wave of shock bolt through her. The hint of stiffening that never really formed into resistance. Then her lips softened, and she made a soft sound that was like manna for his starved senses. Her arms closed around his shoulders.

He groaned, took her mouth more fully, absorbing the taste of her. His hands swept down her spine, caught her hips. She arched against him, her breath nearly a sob as she tore her mouth from his, pressing her lips against his neck.

Mel struggled for sanity. "I can't think when you touch me."

His chest rumbled. "Maybe we do better when we don't think." He stepped backward, coming up against the side of the Jeep, pulling her easily with him. The ocean swept in and out far below them, the Jeep shading them from the road, and his hand covered her breast.

Mel gasped, moaned, felt fire streak through her as his thumb roved over, around her tight nipple. "Luke—"

"Shh." His lips burned down her throat. He flipped open the top button on her dress. His arm around her waist urged her closer, his hard thigh slipping between hers as he took more of her weight. His hand moved against her breast. Another button escaped.

And, oh, she wanted his hands on her. It was insane, it was foolish, it was—

He slid his hand inside her dress, tipping the cup of her bra down, finding her bare flesh.

It was perfect.

Her heart raced, need twining deep inside her with every brush of his fingers. And it wasn't enough. She knew it.

He knew it.

His mouth found hers, both hands working on the buttons that stretched from the modest scooped neck to her waist, and freed them all. He pushed it from her shoulders, his eyes burning over her. Her skin tightened, seemed fit to burst from the way her breasts swelled under his gaze. "Beautiful," he murmured.

The dress dipped to her waist, caught by the press of their bodies against each other. He lowered his head, caught one peak between his lips, and Mel's head fell back, staring unseeingly at the pure blue overhead, wildness sliding into her bloodstream, expanding, bubbling.

She arched against him, mindless with need, and heard the rough caress of his breath, felt the strength of his hands cradling her against him, the hard press of his body in return. "Luke...I...Dr. Hugo said—"

"It's okay," he promised, seeming to know what she wanted, what she needed, without words. "Forget Hugo." His thigh was hard against her, notched high between her thighs. His hand slid over her breasts, over the hard swell of her abdomen, the panties that clung to her moist flesh. Then he kissed her, slid his fingers over her, inside her.

Her mind screamed his name, and she convulsed against him, endless pleasure streaking from nerve ending to nerve ending, from the ends of her waist-length hair to the toes curling against her leather sandals.

And when her strength gave out, he was there, holding her, taking all of her weight, soothing in the wake of exciting, calming in the path of inflaming. She could feel his arousal, felt fire in her cheeks in the face of her utterly wanton behavior. "I'm sorry."

His chest rumbled again. "You're kidding, right?"

He tilted back her head, looking at her. His eyes narrowed. "You're not."

She blushed even harder.

A strange look crossed his face. He touched the corner of her lips, then pressed a gentle kiss to her forehead. "You're so damned sexy you kill me, Mel."

"But I...you didn't—"

His lips tilted crookedly. "So? You did, and that's enough for me."

He adjusted her clothing, started doing up her buttons and laughed softly when she sank her teeth into her lip, hauling in her breath on a hiss as his knuckles brushed her hypersensitive breasts.

"Enough for now. Until next time," he amended.

Then he helped her back into the Jeep, leaving her to silently wonder if she was more comforted or frightened by his seeming certainty that there *would* be a next time.

Chapter 11

Mel stared at the notation she'd made on the appointment calendar spread out in front of her on the desk. Only a day had passed since she'd seen Dr. Hugo.

Since her madness at the hands of Luke Trahern.

She'd done it. Made the appointment for the ultrasound with Dr. Hugo's contact in San Diego. Now she just needed to have the courage to tell Luke, knowing that he'd fully, rightfully, expect to accompany her.

She tossed aside the pen she held when she realized she was chewing on the plastic end of it. It rolled, coming to a stop against her daily muffin basket.

Since their picnic the past weekend when Luke came upon them, Mel hadn't been over to visit April. It was only a few days, of course, but for April, each day counted. She sighed, turning her chair until she could see out the window. It had been the same way with

Nicky. Every day was more precious than the last, a gift in a life that was destined to be far too brief.

In Nicky's case there'd been no choice, no miracle surgery that could come along and save the day. She'd known that early on when the results of the oh-so-standard, thoroughly innocuous prenatal tests started coming back with disturbing results. Then had come the early ultrasound, followed by the damning amnio, and Jonathan's flat insistence that she get rid of the baby that would be born nowhere near perfect.

A sharp nudge from a little foot or a head or a hand caught her attention and she rubbed her hand gently over the spot, soothing the babies even as she pushed away the memories of her pregnancy with Nicky.

It seemed her life was filled with areas about which she didn't want to think too deeply. Nicky. Her parents. *Luke.*

His name sighed through her thoughts. She still couldn't believe what had occurred between them on the road outside of town. Traffic was nearly nil on the road, but that didn't mean that someone might not have passed by, wondered, speculated over what the two people on the far side of the Jeep were doing.

Her cheeks ran hot. If only *she* could forget what they'd done. Forget the feel of his hands on her. Forget the feel of her hands on *him*.

"Chicken, what's got your mind in a twist?"

Mel whirled around in her chair, facing the door and Maisy, who stood there. Guilt suffused her, as if her friend had divined her unwholesome thoughts. "Excuse me?"

"You ordered seventy-two pounds of horseradish

and one pound of laundry soap on your monthly order with Nielsen's.''

''I did?''

Maisy nodded. ''Don't worry. I fixed the numbers. Nielsen called me, seeing how we don't use seventy-two pounds of horseradish in a year, much less a month.''

''Sorry.''

Maisy came into the office and sat down. ''You want to tell me what's got you so dithered? Or do I even need to ask?''

Mel studied Maisy for a moment, and then simply took the bull by the horns. ''Why didn't you warn me that Luke was coming back to the island?''

''And give you a chance to run away again?''

''I wouldn't have.''

''Chicken,'' Maisy said, and sighed, ''don't kid a kidder. I love you dearly, but you've been running since you left San Francisco. I understand why, I do. But it's time you started living life again. Those babies you're carrying deserve a mama who is living in the present with them, not in the past with a sad memory.''

''You don't even like Luke.''

Maisy didn't jump up and deny it. ''I don't like arrogant doctors butting into my business.''

''That's what Jonathan did.''

Maisy nodded. ''And I let him use April like some great pincushion for way too long. A thing to be studied, experimented on, rather than a child to be cherished. It's what Jason Frame tried to do, too, but I think his motives were truer than your ex-husband's. Even though he sent Luke initially to do the hard work of getting around me, I think he has April's welfare at heart, while Dr. Deerfield considered her a specimen.''

''Maisy,'' Mel sat forward, clasping her suddenly unsteady hands together atop the desk. She looked at her friend. ''Are you considering it? Allowing Luke to evaluate April's condition?''

Maisy didn't answer for a long while. ''Maybe,'' she finally allowed. ''Well, that's not what I'm here to yammer about, anyway. I want to know if you've told Luke about all that? About your life with that man?''

Mel's heart charged with hope at Maisy's admission. But she knew better than to run with the issue, force the woman to make her choices at anyone's pace other than her own. Though she wanted to. Badly. ''*That man* presumably being Jonathan. And no, I haven't. I can't.''

Maisy's eyes were kind behind the impatience. ''Why not?''

''I don't want his pity, Maisy.''

''Good grief, chicken, who says you'll have it? You think he hasn't had his share of loss, of grief? You can see it in the man's eyes. All you have to do is look. Even faded old peepers like mine could see it.''

Mel had looked. But every time she did, something about the man drew her, and she couldn't afford to be *drawn*. ''He lost his little sister when they were young,'' she admitted.

''There you go, then. Tell the man, Mel. He might surprise you.''

''And what good would that do me? He lives in Arizona, for heaven's sake. And I—''

''Have been hiding out on Turnabout for too long, now.''

Mel went stiff with shock.

''Oh, relax, chicken. I've gotten as much out of your being here as you have. Probably more. There's nobody on this island that I'd have trusted Maisy's Place to more than you, and it's let me spend far more time with April. I've been entirely selfish in that regard. You remind me so much of Tessa, and I really made a mess with her. I don't want the same thing happening with you.''

Mel's thoughts were reeling. ''You're one of the least selfish people I know. Where is all this coming from?''

''I had breakfast with Luke today.''

Mel gaped. ''You...what?''

''Actually,'' Maisy looked a tad defiant, ''if I'm gonna be strictly honest, and it seems I'm feeling like it this morning, April and I had breakfast with him. I invited him. And I think you might be confusing Jonathan's behavior with Luke's. Maybe we both have been.''

''Who's Jonathan?''

Mel nearly jumped out of her skin. She went from staring at Maisy to staring at Luke, who'd appeared out of nowhere in her doorway. Her mouth worked but no sound emerged. ''Nobody'' finally came out. And it was true. Jonathan *was* nobody to her now. She was barely the same person she'd been when they'd been married. She owed most of the credit for *that* to the red-haired woman sitting across her desk who was giving her a disgusted look.

Well, just because she owed Maisy her very sanity for providing a place for her on Turnabout when Mel hadn't been sure whether living was preferable to dying didn't mean that she now had to bare all to Luke Trahern.

She'd bared plenty already, thank you very much.

The man in question was studying her as if he didn't believe the answer, either.

"I made the ultrasound appointment," she said, certain that it would be more than enough to distract him.

"When?"

"Tomorrow at four. They're fitting me in at the end of the appointment schedule."

"You'll have to take Diego's early run, otherwise you might be late," Maisy said. She pushed out of the chair and sidled past Luke, giving him a sniff. "Make sure she eats before you make the crossing, or she'll probably make a mess of those expensive shoes you wear."

He watched Maisy depart then entered the office on his "expensive" shoes—a thoroughly dilapidated pair of athletic shoes. "Your eating habits are a frequent tune of hers. Who's Jonathan?"

"Don't you have something to do other than disturb my workday?"

"Why?" A whisper of a smile crossed his lips. "When this is such a fun way to spend a vacation."

Mel frowned at the reminder of Luke's seeming reason for coming to Turnabout. Jonathan had never wanted to take vacations. Unless it combined business and pleasure, with an emphasis on business, he had no time for it. "Tomas takes divers out several times a week. You should go with him. The water is great this time of year.''

''I'm not interested in strapping a tank on my back and disappearing under a ton of water. Thanks anyway.''

Amusement was unexpected but undeniable. He looked as if he'd rather have his toenails peeled off than go scuba diving. ''Not your idea of fun. Then what is?''

''Working on the '69 Camaro I'm restoring,'' he said easily.

She narrowed her eyes, visualizing. ''I can almost picture you playing grease monkey.'' With his lean, bristled cheeks, too-long hair and his clothes that suited him but were hardly *GQ*-worthy, he looked big and tough and just a little bit rough. Wrenches sticking out his back pocket didn't seem too far a visual stretch.

''There's no play about it,'' he assured. ''You're talking about a man and his car. Serious matter.''

''Well, as long as you don't crush your fingers under an engine block and end the career that probably pays for your little hobby, I say go for it.''

One moment there was laughter in his sapphire eyes and the next there was nothing. His expression closed, utterly and completely. ''What time does Diego make his run in the morning?''

Feeling rather like the rug had been pulled out from under her, Mel wavered a moment. ''Um, around ten, usually.'' She didn't bring up the subject that they'd probably be stuck in San Diego overnight, as Diego's last run was shortly after the time of her scheduled appointment.

"Okay." He nodded. "I'll meet you at the dock in the morning."

Then he disappeared as silently as he'd appeared.

"Well," Mel said to the plant growing on the window ledge behind her. "Well."

There was no real reason to feel piqued at his abrupt departure, yet she did. But she also couldn't deny the curiosity that swelled inside her. Curiosity and... concern.

And beneath it all, a stone-cold fear of what the ultrasound might reveal.

Her anxieties were alive and well when Tomas dropped Mel off at the dock the next morning. The sight of Luke already there surprised her. He and Diego were bent over the mechanical workings of Diego's ugly boat and neither man made so much as an acknowledgment of her presence when she walked up behind them.

"Ahem." Her eyes drifted over the boat. Over the sight of Luke. He wore a plain white shirt tucked into faded blue jeans. She swallowed and focused on Diego, who was probably fifty but looked eighty and provided a much safer view. "Is there a problem with the motor?"

Both men straightened and turned to her. "No," Luke said. He picked up a faded red rag and began wiping black goop from his hands. "Not a thing." He'd shaved, revealing a slash of a dimple that showed when his lips tilted. "So if you were hoping you could still get out of this, you're wrong."

"I made the appointment, didn't I?"

At her defensive answer, Luke just gave her a knowing look and finished leisurely wiping the grease from his hands. It'd felt good to mess with an engine again. Even though the '69 was sitting in his garage waiting for him whenever he wanted to tinker, he hadn't done even much of that over the past half year.

He finished with the red cloth and tossed it on top of one of the heavy wooden crates that were lined up on the dock, then helped Mel onto the craft. The boat looked as if it could transport a few dozen people at best. Today, half the space was filled with cargo.

Mel stepped around an oversize box fastened shut with twine and tape, and chose a single seat among the unpadded benches marching across the forward section. She plopped her large purse on the deck near her feet.

After retrieving his small gym bag from the dock, Luke sat across from her and stretched out his legs. "I like the dress. You look good in white." Truth was, Melanie Summerville looked good in just about anything. Particularly her honey-tinted skin.

She smoothed her hand over the dress, only to cut the gesture short. "Thank you."

"Reminds me of the dress you wore on the beach. Why *were* you wearing that kind of dress on that night? It was cold out." And he'd warmed her. And had wondered ever since what had been so significant about that night to her. The desire to know had long outgrown simple curiosity.

"Too bad I hadn't chosen woolens to wear," she said. "Then you'd have been able to walk right by me with no qualms whatsoever."

The deck vibrated underneath their feet, and with a

slight lurch, the boat began moving. He focused on her pregnant belly. "And miss this?"

"As if you wouldn't jump at the chance for *this* to have never occurred."

He watched her for a long moment. Then he sat forward, resting his arms on his legs, his loosely clasped hands belying his complete urge to shake her. "I don't know who set that standard for you," he said quietly. "The guy who was responsible for your other pregnancy, I imagine. But don't compare the two of us. I stand by my responsibilities."

"And every woman just loves to hear that she's a *responsibility*."

"I'd stand by you even without the babies." He meant it, too. Sooner or later she'd understand that when he'd said she was his focus now, he'd meant it.

She looked startled. And impossibly yearning, though he knew she'd spit nails before admitting it.

Then, as he could have predicted, her lips tightened and she looked away. "Easy enough for you to say given the situation."

The boat picked up speed, and she was facing the wind head-on. It blew her hair away from her fine features, her long, lovely neck. Want, never far, was a steadily tightening fist inside him. "What's it gonna take for you to trust me, Mel?"

Her lashes swept down, hiding her dark eyes. "I don't know," she finally admitted in a voice so low he had to work hard to hear.

But he did hear. "Well. At least that's honest." Then he sat back again, stretching his arms across the empty bench on either side of him.

They were silent the entire rest of the trip. By the time they made port, Mel seemed glad to escape as he settled up their fares with Diego. When he joined her, she'd signaled for one of the cabs that were parked nearby. He helped her into the rear of the vehicle, then pleased himself by sitting closer to her than she wanted him to.

They still had a few hours before her appointment. "Do you have a place you like to go for lunch?"

She lifted a shoulder and shook her head.

"Nowhere?"

"I come from San Francisco, not San Diego."

"Yeah, but when you come to the mainland, you must—"

"I don't."

"No favorite places?"

"Don't come to the mainland."

Luke looked at her. She was staring out the side window and had inched closer to the opposite side of the car, in fact, as if she needed to put as much space between them as humanly possible.

One step forward, twenty steps back, he thought, and struggled for patience until he had a good, tight grip on it. "You've stayed on Turnabout the entire time you've lived there?"

"Yes."

"Why?"

She finally moved her shoulders in irritation. "Because I felt like it, okay?"

"Hey, pal, the meter's running whether we're moving or not." The cabby's rusty voice interrupted them.

Luke sighed and gave the address of the medical

center. Once they got there, he figured it was a good bet there would be eateries within easy distance.

Whether she liked it or not, he was going to take care of her, and their babies.

Then he reached over and gently but insistently loosened the white-knuckled fist she'd made around the strap of her leather bag and took her hand in his.

He felt as if he'd scored a winning touchdown when she slowly relaxed and curled her fingers around his.

Chapter 12

Mel's tension grew with every minute that ticked by. Though she tried to hide it from Luke, she knew she was doing a miserable job of it.

She'd choked down some of the lunch he'd ordered for her in a cute little café down the block from the medical center only because she hadn't wanted him to make a federal case out of it had she refused.

But now, as they sat in the cool white-tiled room and waited for the technician to come in and run the ultrasound, Mel felt as if her nerve endings were slowly but surely eating right through her skin.

"Couldn't they at least try to stay on time?" She looked at the clock for the umpteenth time. It was half past the hour of her appointment. "What is it with you medical people that you think your time is more valuable than anybody else's?"

Slouched on a metal stool, Luke looked thoroughly

relaxed and at home in the sterile environment. She realized that he generally looked at home wherever he was, and envied him the ability.

"Because we *are* better than anybody else," he answered smoothly.

Her jaw loosened. She shot him a look, only to see the amusement in his face. "Hilarious," she grumbled.

He slid the rolling stool over to the side of the inclined table where she sat, a ubiquitous paper gown and sheet covering her more than adequately. Still she felt practically naked with Luke there, and it was just one more reason her nerves were spiking.

She nearly jumped out of her skin when he grabbed her hand, much as he had in the cab. "Appointments get off track," he said calmly. "It's what happens when you're dealing with people. Some patients take longer than others. It has nothing to do with establishing some supposed superiority over the lesser mortals."

"Even though we *are* lesser mortals," she added.

His lips tilted. "Smart aleck."

Her stomach dipped, hollowed out. He was far easier to resist when he was…oh, who was she kidding? He was *never* easy to resist. That was the whole problem.

Fortunately, the technician arrived then—a harried-looking young woman who perked up almost immediately when she laid eyes on Luke. One lazy half smile from him and the girl was all sweetness and light.

Mel was so annoyed that she forgot to be nervous, and before she knew it, the ultrasound was well underway, images of her babies—yes, there were two—on the screen that the technician rolled close for viewing.

"These little ones like to have their picture taken," the girl said, and within minutes it seemed, the process was complete, and Mel was holding a snapshot of the black-and-white images. "Everything looks good."

Mel stared at the photograph, studying every line, every curve. Bone-deep relief numbed her. She was vaguely aware of the technician exchanging a bunch of medical jargon with Luke before departing, and highly aware of the warmth of Luke's body next to her as he sat on the table beside her.

"A boy and a girl," he said. He leaned forward, peering at the photo. "Or so it appears. Have any names in mind?"

She was shaking. "I didn't let myself think about names."

He looked at her, and she realized how closely they sat. She could see the fine web of lines arrowing out from the corners of his eyes and the thin, dark ring of near black that surrounded his sapphire irises. There were even a few strands of silver hair at his temples, barely noticeable among the thick, dark waves of hair.

"Why not?" he asked.

Would their daughter and son have his coloring? Or would they be fair like she was? Or maybe they would have combined traits—fair hair and blue eyes or rich brown hair and equally dark brown eyes. "What?"

A faint smile played about his lips. "You're looking a little glazed, Mel."

Her cheeks warmed, yet she felt powerless to find her equilibrium. "The babies looked fine."

His expression gentled. "Yes." He brushed his fingers through her hair, then tucked his knuckles under her chin. "You want to tell me why you were afraid they wouldn't?"

It was that kindness in him again. She shook her head, blinking back tears, and slipped off the table, paper gown and sheet rustling. "I need to dress."

"And I guess that's my cue to step outside." He stood but didn't head for the door. "It'd help to talk about it, Mel."

"Counseling 101?"

"Grandfather 101. A burden shared is a burden lessened."

Mel's teeth worried the inside of her lip. Her head knew the truth of his words, but a lifetime of living the opposite seemed impossible to overcome. Even after Nicky's death, Jonathan hadn't shared his thoughts or his grief with Mel, and he'd made it clear he hadn't wanted to hear hers, either.

"Is that what you tell all your patients when you're saving them?"

A shadow came and went in his eyes. "Maybe." He finally reached for the door. "I'll be in the waiting room." He left, closing the door quietly after him.

Mel picked up the photograph and studied it for a moment. Then she smoothed her hand over her belly and dressed.

On her way out, she learned that Luke had already taken care of the bill. But he was in the waiting room when she made her way through the maze of corridors the large office possessed.

He stood as soon as she entered the room and tucked his hand under her elbow as if he'd been doing it all their lives, walking with her from the office and out into a lovely California sunset. "I called for a cab. It should be here any minute."

They stopped on the sidewalk outside the gleaming glass doorway. Palm trees lined the exterior of the building and lush plants with vivid scarlet flowers filled brick planters nearly to overflowing. As far as medical complexes went, it seemed particularly welcoming. Too bad the exam rooms were almost cold in comparison. "What's your clinic like in Arizona?"

The look he shot her was indecipherable. "Sunquest?"

"It's in Phoenix, isn't it?"

"North of it a little. But, yeah, still part of the metro area."

"What's it like there?"

"This time of year? Hotter 'n hell."

"I meant the clinic."

"It's well cooled by the best AC money can buy."

"And you call me a smart aleck."

"Birds of a feather."

A cab pulled smoothly to the curb in front of them. "Another truism from Grandfather 101?"

He smiled faintly and opened the taxi door for her. "Sunquest sits on about five square miles overlooking the city. The property was deeded over to the clinic nearly fifty years ago by a grateful family. Jason is the third—and best—administrator the place has had." He followed her into the cab and pulled the door shut.

"And you?"

"Have no interest in administration." His faint smile took the sting from the flat statement before he leaned forward and spoke quietly to the driver.

Mel shifted, trying to get more comfortable with two babies jockeying for position. Given Luke's seeming dedication to force food upon her at every possible juncture, she was surprised when the cab did not deposit them at a restaurant. And she was struck silent when it did deposit them at the posh entrance of a resort hotel.

"No comments?" Luke paid the driver.

"We have to stay somewhere. Unless we were able to find a charter to take us up to Turnabout, Diego's last run was an hour ago." She was almost proud of the nonchalance in her tone. The hotel she'd thought to stay at was in her budget, while this place most certainly was not. Though she was hungry, she was also exhausted. Asserting her independence just then seemed more than she could manage.

And she was very much aware that she had deliberately chosen not to discuss the need for overnight accommodations with him. He'd obviously known, though, given the small bag he'd brought.

Would he expect to share a room with her?

Did she have the strength to resist him if he did?

He took her big leather purse from her and handed it, along with his small gym bag, to the bellman. Then he ushered her through the entry into what seemed more like a beautiful tropical forest than a hotel lobby.

Jonathan would have sailed straight to the concierge, fully expecting his every wish to be catered to and never giving Mel a second thought. He would have his needs attended to and, in Jonathan's mind, that meant that Mel was supposed to be satisfied, as well.

Luke, however, found a nicely cushioned chair and

nudged Mel into it. He even scared up a little decorative pillow that he tucked at the small of her back, alleviating some of the pressure that seemed her constant companion these days. Then he ambled in that loose-jointed way of his over to registration, and managed to look just as purposeful in his movements as Jonathan ever had when he was striding the halls of the hospital, his half-dozen sycophants trotting dutifully along.

Mel closed her eyes. Why was she having so much trouble keeping thoughts of the past out of her mind? Thinking about Jonathan wasn't so awful; she'd long ago come to terms with the fact that he'd married her without loving her. But thoughts of her marriage invariably turned to thoughts of Nicky, and she could hardly bear to go there.

A fine shiver of recognition had her opening her eyes in time to see Luke approach.

All her anxiety, curiosity, anticipation of what room arrangement he would expect coalesced into a ticking bomb. One that exploded when he stopped in front of her chair and held out his hand to help her stand. "I'm not sleeping with you," she blurted. Fire spread through her face right up to the roots of her hair.

"At least you didn't say 'never.'" He handed her a little envelope that contained a keycard. "Relax. It's a suite."

The wind went right out of her sails. She saw his lips tilt and knew he was amused. With no alternative, however, Mel accompanied him to the suite.

And what a suite it was. Every bit as fine as anything Jonathan or her father would have demanded. She barely had time to see that her leather bag had already been placed in one of the enormous bedrooms when there was a discreet knock at the door. She went out to find Luke directing two young men from room service who were bearing a linen-covered table.

Luke must have spotted her hovering in the doorway of her bedroom. "Outside or in?"

"Out," she said faintly.

He nodded, and the tray was set up on the palm-shaded terrace. She watched him sign the check and accompany the two waiters back to the door. Whatever he was saying to them had both young men chuckling as they left.

Then he closed the wide door and looked at her. She still hadn't moved.

"Something wrong?"

"Why did you arrange room service?"

"Because you're exhausted and I'm starved. Now, are we going to go out and enjoy the meal and the sunset or do we have to debate it?" His gaze didn't leave her face as he unbuttoned the cuffs of his shirt and folded them up his arms.

"Is that what I do?"

"What you do is make sure both of us know that you make your own decisions."

She absorbed that. He said no more but merely waited, as if it *were* completely up to her whether or not she went out onto the terrace that was fairly steeped in a romantic setting. He didn't grow impatient and tell her she was behaving like a fool, even though she knew she was more than halfway there.

He was kind and he was patient, and in that moment,

that very moment, she felt that same awesomely intimate connection as she had that night on the beach. As if he had looked into her soul and recognized something familiar there.

"Mel?" He held out his hand.

She swallowed, following her instinct rather than her fear, and put her hand in his. And out to the terrace they went. He made sure she was comfortably seated in the cushioned iron chair—even going inside to find another small round pillow that would help her back—before sitting himself, and her throat tightened.

He began removing silver domes, setting them aside, and she bit her lip. All of her favorites. From a sliced avocado and shrimp salad to strawberries and whipped cream. There was even a frosty chocolate milkshake. "You've been talking to Maisy."

"Does that bother you?" He uncovered his own plate, which contained a mammoth-size hamburger and fragrant, golden French fries.

Was she bothered that he'd been interested enough to not only find out what her preferences were but to indulge her? It was the first time in her life that a man had done such a thing.

Willing herself not to bawl like a baby, she busied herself by smoothing the linen napkin on what little lap she still possessed. "No," she said huskily. "It was very—" she remembered just in time that he never appreciated the word *kind* being applied to him "—thoughtful of you. Thank you."

He studied her for a moment. "You're welcome." Then he reached for a fancy little bottle of ketchup and dumped it over his fries.

Her heart continued skipping every few beats, but she finally managed to follow his lead and begin eating. The food was as delicious as it appeared, but by the time she made it to the silver bowl of plump strawberries, she was positively replete.

The sun was a brilliant orange disk as it sank toward the sea. The breeze was balmy, and from somewhere nearby they could hear the faint strains of music and laughter. All in all, it was a nearly perfect evening. When he suggested a walk on the beach, she mindlessly agreed.

So they headed down the three steps to the smooth beach. Mel slipped off her shoes and felt her stomach dip a little when he took them from her. "Easier than having to find them later," he said.

Which naturally reminded her of the night on the beach when they'd searched for her sandals. After they'd made love.

They walked near the water's edge, where the wet sand was cool and packed. Somewhere along the way, he looped his fingers through hers. When his steps slowed and finally stopped, she stopped, too, and they watched the sun give its last gasp of daylight and finally disappear.

"Hard to get tired of watching that." His voice was quiet.

"What kind of sunsets do you have in Arizona?" How often did he take time from his schedule to stop and watch one?

"Spectacular ones. Sometimes the entire sky looks like it's been set on fire. Then the fire goes out and the city lights go on for as far as you can see."

She wondered if he was even aware of the arm he'd slipped around her shoulder. *She* was excruciatingly aware of the weight of it, the warmth of it. The fact that his fingertips grazed her upper arm, the fact that his scent was consuming her senses. "Sounds like you miss it. You've been away for a few weeks, now. Are you anxious to get back?"

He made a low sound. Of assent, dissent, she wasn't sure.

She swallowed. "Most people find vacations thoroughly enjoyable, but toward the end, returning home has a particular lure, also."

"Vacations." He let out a short breath, not quite a laugh. "Is that how you discovered Turnabout? Headed there on vacation and decided to stay?" His fingers drifted up her shoulder, sliding through her hair.

Shivers danced down her spine. "No, I knew of Turnabout long before I went there."

Chapter 13

Luke shot her a quick look. "How's that?"

Mel realized too late what she'd admitted. It was because he was touching her, she thought somewhat desperately. He touched her, and her brain shut off. "Turnabout isn't well-known, of course. The Turns prefer it that way. There always seems to be enough tourism to keep the local economy moving along, but not enough to—"

"Ruin it."

She nodded. "Yes."

"That still doesn't tell me how you learned about it."

She should have known he wouldn't be derailed from the question. "I, um, I met Maisy when she took April to San Francisco for treatment. I lived there."

"Right. One of the few things you've almost told me."

"Luke—"

"I don't need to know all the details of your past," he said abruptly. "Unless they affect the here and now, your past is your business."

Unfortunately, they both knew her past was most definitely affecting the here and now.

"But I still want you to marry me. I still want to be there for our children."

Her knees felt weak. "That doesn't require marriage."

"It does in my book." He caught her head in his big hand and pressed a kiss to her temple. "Grandfather 101."

Then, just when she was a mental mess at the proof that he hadn't given up the marriage business, he slid his hand down from her shoulder, caught up her hand in his, and turned back toward the hotel. "Let's get you back inside before you get chilled. I don't have a jacket with me to keep you warm."

She didn't need his jacket to be warm. She only needed him. The disturbing thought settled in her mind for the walk back and stayed there even after she excused herself for the night and closed herself into the bedroom.

It was still a little early, but remaining in the living room with him represented more danger than she could handle. So she showered and partly dried her hair, using the blow dryer provided in the well-appointed bathroom. She wouldn't have minded a soak in the enormous tub, but was afraid that once she got in, she'd be unable to get back out.

Her nightgown was short and lightweight and had

taken up little room in her oversize purse along with her change of clothes for the next day. Luke had been right that the evening would be cool. But she didn't want to shut out the fresh air drifting through the terrace door, so she wrapped herself in one of the plush robes that hung in the closet, again courtesy of the hotel.

With nothing left to do, though, Mel still felt no real inclination to go to bed. She tried the television, but it failed to hold her interest. She called the inn and reached Tomas, who assured her that all was well. As usual, Maisy had spent the day with April.

She even went so far as to listen against the door, trying to hear whether or not Luke had retired for the night. But the door was too solid.

Disgusted with herself, she yanked open the door and sagged a little at finding the living area empty. The door across from her bedroom was closed. Luke had obviously done just what she had. She only hoped he was having better luck settling in for the night.

While they'd been out on the beach, room service had cleared away the remains of their dinner. But they'd left behind the bowl of strawberries and the whipped cream. They were nicely nestled in a crystal bowl of melting ice on the gleaming granite bar, and Mel took both the berries and the cream and carried them over to the deep sofa.

She stretched out, her back propped up against the arm of the sofa, and began nibbling away. Luke had left the ultrasound photograph on the cocktail table and she leaned over and picked it up, studying it.

And that's how Luke found her when he opened his

door a few minutes later. He'd been intent on finding a cold beer somewhere. 'Cause God knows he was having a helluva time overlooking the fact that Mel was only a handful of steps and a door away.

But the sight of her told him that it wasn't beer he really wanted. It was her.

Her robe had parted where her long legs were crossed one over the other, and for a long while, he let himself look at the shapely limbs. High on her creamy thighs he could see the gleaming edge of dark blue fabric and tortured himself with the immediate vision of satin sliding over her soft skin.

His hands curled.

He didn't doubt that he could get her into his bed. He knew that his touch was as potent for her as hers was for him. But somewhere along the way—maybe from the very first—he'd begun to want more.

So he sucked in a long breath, yanked the tails of his shirt loose from his jeans to hide the predictable effect she had on him, and cleared his throat as he walked into the salon. "Can't sleep?"

She sat bolt upright, the two bowls tumbling out of her grasp. She grabbed for them quickly, only to end up with a hand doused in whipped cream. The bowls hit the floor, and strawberries bounced across the thick ivory carpet. "Great," she grumbled. "Stop sneaking around."

He smiled faintly, conscious of the awareness in her eyes and the pink color riding her cheeks. They were having babies together, they were adults, and they were alone in a hotel suite that seemed fit for honeymooners.

If he were a nicer man he would have arranged for

completely separate rooms. Instead, he was wondering how he could get into her head and keep outta her bed. And wondering why he was bothering. Making love with her was something they both wanted, whether or not they chose to admit it.

"Stay put," he said. "I'll clean up."

She leaned back once more, watching as he hunted down strawberries and tossed them back into the silver bowl. He found the last just under the edge of the cocktail table and straightened, on his knees next to the sofa and the hand she was holding aloft, being careful not to smear any of the whipped cream onto the sofa. It was already covering her fingertips, and there was a white smear on her knee and the hem of her nightgown that was even more visible, thanks to the way she'd jumped when he'd startled her.

Hell. "Go to bed *now,* Mel."

Her eyes widened, her lips looking soft and probably tasting sweeter than the cream. "Or what?"

"Or come to bed in mine."

She hesitated. He could see her pulse beating in her throat. It took every inch of willpower he possessed to keep his hands where they were. *Off* her.

Her legs moved, slipping from the couch and her knee—the one with the tiny smear of whipped cream— brushed against his elbow.

Good, he thought. Go, and go fast. Because he was at the edge of sanity.

Her hair slid forward over her shoulder, slightly damp, utterly touchable, grazing his wrist.

"The dress," she said softly. "The white one. From that night on the beach. It was my son's favorite. I wore it for his last birthday.'' She hesitated, her gaze on her whipped-creamed fingers.

Last birthday.

She hadn't had a pregnancy that hadn't made it to term.

She'd had a child who hadn't lived to adulthood.

Luke damned the volatile situation. He gently took her hand, wiping it clean on his shirt before he did something really stupid, like lick it off. Then he put his arms around her and carried her to her bed.

He settled her, robe and all, in the middle of the wide bed that showed signs of her having tried to occupy it earlier. He pulled the soft blanket over her then sat on the side of the bed. She didn't seem to want to let go of his hand, and that was okay, too. ''How old was he?''

''Nearly five. His name was Dominic.'' She was looking at their linked hands. ''I called him Nicky and he was everything to me. I saw in a baby-name book once that it meant 'belonging to the Lord.' I figure it must be true, because according to all the doctors, it was a miracle he was ever born.'' She turned on her side, away from him, but she still held his hand. ''Much less that he lived past his first year.''

''What happened?''

''He died.''

The scientist in him demanded details.

The man in him wanted to protect her from them.

The father he was going to be fell somewhere in between, but for now, the man won out.

She'd finally shared. And he finally understood the

fears she must have had as a constant companion since discovering he'd left her pregnant on that fateful night.

"This is why you were hesitant to see Hugo. Because you were afraid what the prenatal tests might show."

"Yes." Her voice was barely a whisper.

"What if they hadn't been in normal ranges? What would you have done?"

"The same thing I did before. Have the baby."

He let out a long breath and studied the slender line of her back. He wondered if there had been somebody beside her while she'd dealt with those decisions the first time. And if there had been, whether she'd been supported. But wondering was all he'd do, just then. If she wanted to tell him about the father, she would.

Maybe she still loved him. The thought was dismal.

"Try to get some sleep," he said after a moment. "We'll catch Diego's first run in the morning." He started to rise, but she tightened her hold on his hand.

"Don't go."

He looked at her. "I don't think my staying is a good idea."

She pushed up on her elbow. "Are you angry with me?"

"No."

She let go of his hand and sat up even more, and her robe parted completely, displaying a satin nightgown every bit as appealing as he'd feared. And it clung lovingly to curves that appealed most of all.

"Then why are you leaving me?"

"Because you don't need a guy like me right now."

"What's that supposed to mean?"

''You're still grieving your son.''

''It was four years ago.''

''Yeah, and you haven't even come close to accepting it.''

Her lashes swept down, hiding her expression. ''You don't know that.''

''You obviously left San Francisco when it happened. You've admitted you haven't been off Turnabout since you went there. You haven't spoken with your parents. You've barely been able to acknowledge your pregnancy. Are you telling me all that is a sign of a woman who's come to terms with a horrible loss?''

She looked wounded. He ran his hand down his face. No matter what he wanted from her, he knew he wasn't good at this. Matters of the heart, matters of the mind. But he wasn't heartless, either, and he didn't know how to help her when he could barely keep his hands off her. ''Look. I'm sorry. It's late. And we're both tired.''

Her lips compressed. ''Of course,'' she finally said quietly. ''You're right.''

She looked to the side of the bed, spotted the light switch and snapped it off. Then she lay back down and pulled the blanket over her shoulders.

He watched her in the dim room.

She'd shared a huge piece of herself with him. But instead of feeling good about it, he felt as if he'd failed.

Again.

He turned and left, pulling the door closed with a click.

Inside, in the darkness, Mel wiped away a tear. She knew she wouldn't sleep that night.

By morning, the proof of that was apparent in the drawn features that looked back at her from the bathroom mirror as she dressed in the peach-colored crinkly dress she'd brought with her.

It was no comfort, whatsoever, that Luke appeared just as weary as she felt when she left the loneliness of her bedroom behind. He was obviously waiting for her, standing at the granite bar, paging through a newspaper. The lines around his eyes seemed deeper, the set of his mouth tighter. He still wore jeans, but he'd traded the white shirt for a black polo. He was gorgeous, and he was about as distant as a person could seem.

''Ready?''

She nodded and he picked up his small bag and headed for the door. Mel tucked the ultrasound photo inside her purse and followed. They stopped off at the casually chic coffee shop located near the lobby, and shared a silent breakfast.

Then it was back down to the port where Mel bought a magazine in a crowded little shop, and Luke seemed lost in his own thoughts while they waited for Diego. Once his boat came into view, and he'd unloaded and they'd boarded, the crossing passed just as silently.

Tomas was waiting with a motor cart when they arrived over an hour later on Turnabout. Mel looked from Tomas to Luke's Jeep that was still parked where he'd left it. But before she could head toward it, Luke had already climbed in and started the engine. Without another look her way, he slowly drove away.

If she'd thought that telling Luke about Nicky would bring them closer, it seemed she'd failed miserably.

The realization that she wanted to be closer to Luke, though, was as much of a shock as anything. It was a distinct problem considering that, sooner or later, he *would* return to Arizona. Whether or not she agreed to be his wife.

Chapter 14

The first thing Mel did when Tomas stopped the cart was go in search of Maisy. She found her at her cottage. As soon as April heard Mel's voice, she tossed off her blanket and hopped up from the rattan couch. She bounded across the room, throwing her arms around Mel's expanded waist.

"Hello, babies," she greeted. "Hello, Mel! Do you really got two babies in there?"

Some of Mel's tension slid away and she laughed. "I really do." She wished she could show April the ultrasound photo and had to content herself with handing it over to Maisy. "A boy and a girl, so I'm told."

April pulled her head back, staring at Mel's belly as if she could see right through to the babies. "Cool."

Mel smiled and ruffled April's curls. "Yeah. Cool."

"So," Maisy set down the photo and propped her

hands on her hips, "I don't suppose you and Dr. Daddy got hitched overnight."

Mel's jaw loosened. "Of course not."

Maisy made a face. "In my day, people who made babies got married. Usually beforehand."

Mel's eyebrows rose. "Is something bothering you?" Maisy had never before made such comments.

"Dr. Hugo wants to marry Grammy," April said into the silence. "I heard him talking to her last night."

"When you were supposed to be sleeping," Maisy pointed out. Her cheeks were almost as red as her hair. "Now, go in and finish the lunch Tomas brought over for you and let Mel and me catch up."

April grinned up at Mel, then walked unerringly over to the table where a sandwich and glass of milk sat waiting.

Mel sat down. "Well? What'd you say to him?"

Maisy waved her hand. "Please. That old coot? He was just trying to get my goat."

"Maisy, Dr. Hugo has loved you ever since I've lived here."

"And he's a Turn."

"So are you."

"In most people's minds, but not for a fact," Maisy corrected. She shook her head. "He shouldn't have asked me. He was just feeling cocky and full of himself, and, well, he just shouldn't have done it, that's all. He knew I'd never agree."

"Just because of that old curse?"

"Don't go sniffing at it, missy."

Mel sighed. She'd defended Maisy's right to believe

in a curse to Luke, but now she was pulling the same disbelieving note that he had. "I'm sorry."

Maisy huffed. But she softened quickly enough. "And you? The test went well?"

She nodded. "There were no abnormalities noted at all." She knew an ultrasound couldn't detect many things, but if this pregnancy had been similar to her first, she would have known it once the ultrasound was complete. "Two babies, two healthy-looking hearts, four active little legs and arms, twenty toes." And the relief of it still made her weak.

"Grammy," April called from the dining table. "Can I spend the night with Lani?"

Maisy frowned. "She's been asking that every night for two weeks," she said in a low voice.

"Maybe you should let her," Mel replied in an equally low voice. They'd had the discussion more than once.

"Maybe you should," April piped in, giggling.

Mel laughed and pushed to her feet. "I'm going to see what kind of mess the office is in."

"No mess, missy. You've only been gone a day. You think this place won't run without you?"

Mel kept her smile in place. The truth was, however, that she knew the inn could run perfectly well without her. It had before she'd arrived. It would, even if she left. That was part of the nature of Turnabout. The nature of life.

Things went on.

Proof of that fact was more than apparent later that evening, as well, as she and Maisy stood in the doorway of the open-air dining area and watched.

Luke and Dr. Hugo were there, looking as if they'd been friends forever. The other guests—two middle-aged married couples and a trio of young women lawyers—were crowded around them. Waving his unlit cigar around expansively, Dr. Hugo seemed to have them in stitches of laughter. Luke seemed to have the unattached females eating from the palm of his hand.

"Well," Maisy muttered, next to her. "They've been at it for two hours, now."

"Tomas said they've gone through several bottles of wine."

"If those fool men want to get snockered, it's no business of mine."

"Right," Mel echoed. She rubbed her hand over a particularly hard kick from one of the babies. "No business."

Maisy huffed yet again. "I'm going to bed," she finally announced. And stomped straight through the dining area where she gave Dr. Hugo an evil eye as she passed.

"Stubborn old woman," he called after her.

"Stubborn old man," she called back just as loudly. The gate that closed off the area from the paths leading to the cottages crashed behind her.

Mel realized Luke was watching her. He raised his wineglass toward her. "Want to join us?"

She eyed the lawyer-ettes clinging to him. "I don't think so."

His lips twisted and when one of the girls—titian-haired and large-breasted—leaned against his shoulder, he turned his attention to her.

Mel spun on her heel and headed toward her office,

slamming the door shut so hard it bounced right back open. Yeah, right, the man wanted to marry her.

He only wanted to do what some pea-brained piece of conscience, drilled into him by an old-fashioned grandfather, told him was right. Marry out of duty?

Well, not her.

No way.

He could sit there with a *dozen* chesty ladies climbing all over him and she didn't care. She didn't!

"Jealous?"

She gasped, turning to see the man in question standing in the doorway. "Hardly," she snapped. "And you're drunk."

"Not anywhere near drunk enough," he said, and came into the office, closing the door far more quietly than she'd done. "Still standing, aren't I? Still awake. Always awake and when I'm not, I wish I was."

She held out a stiff arm. "Just stay over there."

He leaned back against the door and crossed his arms. "Afraid of what'll happen if I get any closer?"

"Your ego is astounding."

"Even if I am right," he nodded, his eyes heavy lidded. It was the only evidence of the wine he'd apparently consumed. "Why are you in your office at this hour? You should be resting somewhere."

"Gestating like the good little woman while you're out carousing?"

His lips tilted. "You won't carouse with me, rightfully so, and you probably don't want me rubbing your feet anymore, 'cause that'll lead to rubbing your calves and your thighs and—"

"Stop."

He did, his expression knowing. "You're thirty-one, with your whole life ahead of you."

"Go back to Dr. Hugo, Luke." Mel sat behind her desk. "You're making no sense whatsoever."

He stepped forward and leaned over her desk. "Maisy's going to change her mind about April, you know. She's almost there."

The possibility sent hope streaking through Mel, even as she cautioned herself against it. "I thought you didn't come to the island this time to talk to Maisy about April."

His sapphire eyes narrowed. "I didn't. I told you. I came 'cause—" he frowned "—'cause Jase said I needed a vacation."

"And how long is that vacation supposed to last?"

"Can't wait to get rid of me?"

She didn't dare tell him how badly she feared the opposite. "You've got work waiting for you at Sunquest. Patients."

His lips twisted. "You'd think so, wouldn't you. Fortunately for them, I'm here. With you."

"Please. A surgeon doesn't exist who doesn't put his patients ahead of everything else in his life."

"You really have it in for us, don't you. All 'cause of your dear ol' daddy."

"I don't want to hear this."

"Why not? The truth hurts, doesn't it."

"What about your truths, Luke? You're not full of life stories that you're dying to share with me. You only want to climb inside *my* head. And the only reason for that is because you think it'll get me to agree to marry you, so that your infernal sense of *duty* is satisfied.''

''You wouldn't want to see what's inside my head, Mel.''

''Well, you never give me a chance, now do you.''

He watched her for a long while. Long enough for her to doubt that he was as inebriated as Tomas had warned. He reached across the desk and drew his fingers down her cheek. Caught her chin when she tried to move away. ''Some nightmares are better left unshared.'' Then he smiled humorlessly and straightened.

''Why are you acting like this?'' She never would have pegged him to have even an ounce too much alcohol.

''Maybe I'm celebrating.''

''Celebrating what?''

''Fatherhood.''

''You have to single-handedly drink several bottles of wine to do that?''

''Considering the alternative? Yeah, maybe so.''

''What alternative?''

''Making love to my babies' mother.'' He waited a beat. ''Nothing to say, Mel?''

She moistened her lips, suddenly feeling very unsure of her footing. ''You were the one who wouldn't stay with me last night.''

''My one good deed lately, and now I get to be punished for it.'' He shook his head. ''Well, that's life.''

''Luke—''

''G'night, Mel. Sleep sweet dreams for us both, why don't you?'' He opened the door and was gone.

For a long while, she sat there, wondering what on

earth had just transpired, feeling it was important, only she couldn't quite figure out why. Eventually, however, she left her office and took the long route back to her cottage.

She could still hear Dr. Hugo's booming laugh and assumed that Luke had returned to the ''party'' as well.

It wasn't until she was lying in her bed, staring up at the dark ceiling, that it finally came to her.

Still awake. And when I'm not, I wish I was. Luke's words.

She knew why her sleep was often fitful.

But why was Luke's?

''Luke, please. Wake up.'' Mel tugged at the sheet, pressing her hand to his darkly bronzed shoulder, shaking him. ''Come on, Luke, how much did you and Dr. Hugo drink last night?'' She shook him again. Harder. Her throat was tight, tears thickening her voice. ''Dammit, wake up!''

He opened one eye. Then the other. Propped himself up on his elbows and gave a slow, feral smile. ''Finally.''

''Oh! Get your mind out of your pants.'' She slid off the bed, yanking at the sheet that was tangled around hips that definitely wore no pants of *any* type at that moment. ''Come on. Wake up. Maisy needs you.''

He fell back against the flat mattress, wincing at the movement. When he opened his eyes next, they were somewhat more clear. ''April?''

Mel shook her head. ''No, Maisy. She's hurt, Luke. Come on!'' She jerked at him, at the sheet, and nearly lost her footing when he sat bolt upright and the sheet flew free from him. He was one-hundred-percent naked.

She gasped, closed her eyes, turned on her heel, looking anywhere but at him.

He made an impatient sound as she heard him moving. "Stop acting like a maiden aunt," he muttered. "You've seen it before."

By moonlight, when she was half-crazed with grief. Not in the cold light of day, when all that gloriously bronzed male flesh was exquisitely revealed. She closed her eyes, but the impression seemed permanently imprinted. She was hardly a prude, but didn't the man know what a swimsuit was? He was tanned... all over.

"Silly girl," he chided softly after a moment, and she felt his hands on her shoulders, turning her to face him. She flushed furiously when her eyes automatically dipped, only to find he'd pulled on a pair of jeans. His eyes were amused when she looked up at him, but at least they looked clear and sober. "Now, what's wrong with Maisy?" He tugged a Hawaiian-print shirt over his shoulders.

Mel gulped, guilt spurring her into motion. "She fell off her stepladder. I'm afraid she might have broken something."

"Did you call Hugo?"

"I...no, I...you were closer." She hurried out the door. "She's in her cottage."

Luke dragged her to a halt when she reached the uneven path. "You walk," he ordered. Then he jogged down the path, turning out of sight as he headed for Maisy's cottage.

She tried. She really did. But she ended up doing more of a hop-skip-walk, and when she arrived, Luke was already ministering to Maisy, who was muttering and cursing colorfully under her breath at her own clumsiness.

"Dratted step stool," she said, and glared at the old metal contraption that lay on its side nearby. As if the thing had deliberately failed in order to cause her problems. "Hugo keeps telling me to stay off the thing. I should have him pitch it off the cliff! Where is that infernal man, anyway? Doesn't he know there're people around who need him? Suppose he's away somewhere sleeping it off."

Mel sank down beside Maisy, taking her hand, making soothing noises. But over the woman's orange corkscrews, she glared at Luke. He ignored her, continuing to carefully examine Maisy's left leg.

"I need something to splint it," he murmured, glancing around. "And ice. Then we need to get her to Hugo's clinic. How'd it happen?"

"I found her lying on the floor when I brought by some papers for her to sign."

"Conscious?"

Mel nodded.

"Darn it all, boy, don't talk like I'm not here," Maisy snapped, but her cheeks were pale and Mel knew she was in terrible pain.

The corner of Luke's lips tilted. "You know you can't be too badly off if you can still give me what-for, Maisy."

Mel nearly choked when Maisy flushed and huffed but calmed right down. Luke pushed to his feet and disappeared into Maisy's kitchen—she had a real one even though it was rarely used—and returned a few moments later carrying several flour-sack dish towels that he ripped into strips with fast movements. Then he flipped two movie magazines off a shelf and rolled them into tubes, which he used to brace Maisy's leg before fastening it all up with the cloth strips.

"I know, honey," he murmured, when Maisy groaned as he worked. "It's not a perfect solution, but it'll get you to the clinic."

"Call Lily." Maisy's hand gripped Mel's. "April spent the night with her last night."

Mel looked toward the hall that led to April's room, surprise working through her. Had her conversation with Maisy actually had some effect?

"Get some ice first," Luke suggested as he checked the splint for excessive pressure, then touched Maisy's toes.

Mel knew he was looking for signs of good circulation. She nodded and pushed up on her knees, then to her feet, and hurried into the kitchen. She dumped out a loaf of bread and filled the long bag with ice, then slammed it against the floor a few times until the ice broke up. She also grabbed a bag of frozen peas and carried them back with her. Luke had wrapped a blanket around Maisy's shoulders and elevated her feet. He took the ice and frozen peas and packed them carefully around the splint. Then he took Mel aside and told her to get Tomas quickly, with the stretcher.

"And don't forget to call Lily!" Maisy's voice was shaky as Mel dashed out the door.

The next hour was a blur as they transported Maisy, alternately bickering then tearful, to the clinic where Dr. Hugo—thoroughly sober—took one look at Maisy and turned grim. Between Luke and the older doctor, they got Maisy's fracture set. When Mel phoned Lily, April had insisted on coming to the clinic, too, and before long, it seemed the entire population of Turnabout was crowded into the little building.

It didn't seem to matter to anyone that Maisy had finally dropped into a sedated sleep. They still had to come by and check on her, fuss and tsk and gossip, and generally exclaim what a handy thing it was that Dr. Luke had been so nearby to render immediate aid.

Eventually, however, Dr. Hugo shooed the visitors away, leaving only Mel sitting in the waiting room, wondering what was taking Luke and Dr. Hugo so long back there with a sleeping Maisy. Finally she could wait no longer and went in search of them, only to have Luke appear in the short hallway.

One glance at his face told her more than she wanted to know. "Something *is* wrong. That's why it's been taking you so long."

He rolled his head around, loosening up his neck. "Yeah, but you can consider Maisy's tussle with the stepladder a blessing in disguise."

"What do you mean?"

He was looking at her feet. "Your ankles are swelling."

"I'm carrying twins, remember? They're *always* swollen."

He smiled faintly and took her arm. "Come on. Let's get you settled somewhere other than one of those hard chairs in the waiting room."

"Luke—"

"Let me take care of you first, okay?"

He looked weary, beyond what tying one on the night before should cause, and she wondered again about his sleeping.

Her protests died. And her usual spurt of defensiveness, whenever he tried to tell her what to do, didn't rear its ugly head, either. She just nodded in agreement and saw the flare of surprise in his eyes at her acquiescence.

They were more than halfway to Maisy's Place in the Jeep he'd rented before he spoke again, and then it was only to ask if she'd eaten breakfast that morning.

"Bananas and tuna."

"Well, at least you didn't add peanut butter to it," he said, amused. "Does April eat anything that doesn't have peanut butter on it?"

"Not if she can help it." Mel looked away as remembrance swept through her, sweet and aching. "Nicky loved peanut butter, too."

She felt the weight of his gaze, but he said nothing as he parked the vehicle on a patch of grass at the side of the inn.

Before Mel could even maneuver from the passenger seat, he was there, helping her. "How do you do that?" She felt like a slow-moving blimp, and he was faster than the proverbial speeding bullet.

"I'm not carrying around twins," he said. "Tomas is handling things, I assume."

She nodded. He immediately took her arm and started for the rear of the inn where the paths led off to the private cottages. In her cottage, he nudged her down into her favorite chair, disappeared into her bedroom and returned moments later with two pillows in hand that he tucked under her feet to elevate them even more on the ottoman. Then he moved over to her kitchen area and started rummaging.

His hands on her legs had been brief, but enough to needlessly remind her just how effectively he could use his touch.

She swallowed, willing away the prickles of awareness that plucked at her nerves. "Now, tell me why Maisy's fall is a blessing in disguise."

He turned, a soda in his hand, and popped the top. "You're not drinking these, are you? They're loaded with caffeine." He lifted the can, tilting his head back, and drank deeply.

Her little prickles bloomed into a full-scale body flush. She folded her hands together, looking at her nails. Anything was safer than looking at him. He was better than that old soda-pop commercial during which office workers ogled the hunky laborer during his break.

After a moment, she heard the distinctive crumple of the can, and looked up to see him tossing it into her trash. He raked his hands through his hair and, nudging her legs a bit, sat on the ottoman facing her.

And still he didn't speak. He just looked at her. And dread sliced through her. "Luke?"

Chapter 15

Luke scrubbed his hands down his face, wishing he'd had more than an hour of sleep, wishing he didn't want this woman as much as he did. He knew he'd made an ass of himself the night before, and he wished that hadn't happened, either.

Mostly he wished for a lot of things, none of which were likely to happen.

"We think Maisy has hypertension," he told her. "Hugo's been concerned for a while, trying to monitor her, but—" he spread his hands "—Maisy can be difficult."

"What with April she's had more than enough doctors in her life."

"She said something to that effect," he agreed mildly.

Mel frowned. "I can only imagine what Maisy might have *really* said." She sighed, then nodded. "Okay, she has high blood pressure. She needs to adjust her diet, get more exercise or something.''

"If Hugo's suspicions bear out, she'll need more than that. Her pressure was so high back there we think she might have had some sort of episode before her fall. You said she *was* conscious when you discovered her.''

Her expression fell. "Yes, but she never really said how long she'd been lying there. She's...she's going to be all right, isn't she? April needs Maisy, Luke. If anything happened to her—''

He leaned forward, catching her head between his hands. "Don't borrow trouble. As long as Hugo's got her under his wing for a while, he'll get her stabilized. She'll probably be on meds from now on, but that's hardly catastrophic. The point is that she's going to get the treatment she needs for certain, now. There's no reason to think anything worse will happen.''

"And her leg?''

"It will heal.'' He smoothed his fingers through her silky hair and felt something inside him tighten warningly when her cheek pressed, so briefly, against his palm.

"Thanks for helping her.'' Her voice was husky.

"Why wouldn't I have?'' Setting a fracture was a light-year away from picking up a scalpel. He rubbed his thumb slowly over the fine cheekbone, his gaze on Mel's soft lips. She was maddening, this woman who carried his children. "You didn't call Hugo.''

Her lashes drifted downward. "You were closer.''

"You trusted me. Even after I made an ass of myself last night.''

"Luke—"

He shook his head once. "Admit it, Mel. You came to me because you trusted me."

Her lips pressed together. She looked up at him, mute, her eyes soft. Heat blasted through him.

"So why won't you trust me about everything else?" He could feel her drawing away from him then, mentally if not physically, and damned his tongue. "I haven't told you much about my grandfather."

Though she was still, he could feel the struggle inside her. Whether to stay. Whether to run. He waited, impatience rife within. And finally she gave a faint shake of her head. Apparently *stay* had won out. At least momentarily.

"No," she said. "Obviously he had a large impact on you, though. Grandfather 101 and all. You said he raised you and your sister."

"Bethany. Yeah. She's the one who liked the crusts cut off her toast."

"Where were your parents?"

He *wanted* her curiosity, he reminded himself when a flip dismissal automatically rose in him. "I never knew my dad. Mom never saw a need to marry Bethany's dad, either. Eventually, she didn't see a need for her kids, either, and dumped us off at her dad's ranch in Wyoming."

"I'm sorry."

His hand slid down where her pulse beat like a trapped bird against the smooth column of her throat. "Don't be. We were better off with my grandfather."

Her pupils dilated. "You loved him."

"Does that surprise you?" He smiled ruefully.

"Yeah. Mac Trahern was his name and he was a to-bacco-chewing, bowlegged son of a gun who loved only one woman in his life."

"Your grandmother?"

He nodded. "She died long before Bethany and I went to live with him, though. When Beth died, he was devastated."

Her hand fluttered upward, as if she would have touched him. He very nearly lost his sense when her cool fingertips grazed his jaw then fell away. "You, too," she murmured.

There was no point in denying the obvious. "Mac gave everything he had to put me through medical school. Sold off half his land, his stock. Most people go into debt with student loans for years, but he wouldn't have it. Said I could take care of him in his old age in return."

"Did you?"

"Until he died. Almost a year ago now. I...finally sold his ranch in January."

Her lips sounded out the month.

"The same week I came to Turnabout," he added at the question in her eyes.

"Selling must have been difficult."

"Yeah." He stared at his hands. He'd tried to keep the place going, feeling torn between what little was left of his grandfather's legacy and his own career. The career had won. Only Luke had failed that, too. "Leaving the land there with nobody to care for it was worse," he finally said. "Mac would have hated that. I took a few things from the old house, and sold everything else, lock, stock, and barrel to a neighboring outfit—a huge ranching operation. They'll take care of it the way Mac would have wanted." The way he hadn't.

"What things did you take?"

He shook his head. "His old desk. A clock. Nothing important."

"Important enough for you to keep them. Why the clock?"

"He made it. Sat on his mantel. He had to wind it every day. Took this big old key. Even kept track of the month and day."

Her eyes held a suspicious gleam. "I'm sure your grandfather would have understood your selling, Luke. You just said how he sacrificed for your medical career. Why on earth would he have done that if he'd expected you to follow in his footsteps?"

It was a valid point. One he'd told himself more than once. And he still had a hard time accepting what he'd done. But they were getting off track. He was trying to impress on her that he was a determined man, a focused man. And she *was* his focus.

"People always said how much like my grandfather I was."

"Bowlegged, with chew tucked in your cheek?" She waited a beat. "I don't think so."

"Maybe not in looks or habit, but definitely in temperament. He only loved one woman his entire life. He told me once that he knew the first time he saw my grandmother—even though she was spitting mad at him for letting his prize-winning goat eat its way through her prize-winning county fair brownies—that she was the one for him. It took him a while to convince her of it, but he did. He was a determined man, my grandfather. And so am I. I want you to come back with me to Arizona.''

"So, now you're finally acknowledging the fact that you'll be going back? That your vacation isn't indefinite?''

"You're avoiding an answer, Mel.''

She let out a harried breath. "You know I can't.''

"You mean you won't.''

"Luke—''

"Mel, just *trust* me. I won't hurt you.''

"Nobody ever *tries* to hurt me, it just ends up happening.''

"Is this about losing your son? About his father?'' He knew he was right when her face went white. "What'd he do? Leave you hanging when he found out you were pregnant? I'm not doing that, Mel. I want you to marry me. I want to be there when the babies are born. When they take their first steps, say their first words.''

"Jonathan didn't leave me! I left him.'' She covered her face with her hands. "After Nicky died, I left him. I walked away from our sham of a marriage and I kept walking until I ended up here. On Turnabout with Maisy. She gave me a place to stay, gave me a job to do.''

Luke sat back. He didn't know why it hadn't occurred to him that Mel had been married to Nicky's father. It should have. She was so clear in her position against marriage that he should have realized it came from experience. An experience she flatly refused to repeat.

"How long were you with him?"

"Seven years."

Which meant she'd been hardly more than a teenager. "You were young."

"And he was older," she said tiredly, "and I was besotted and more than happy to be his lovely little trophy."

"Honey, you're far too much your own person to be any man's trophy." He'd seen her in action around the inn. She had a keen eye for organization and an even better gift for making everyone around her feel welcomed, and he'd yet to see her really be pushed around by anyone, even Maisy.

"Well, you must not know me as well as you think you do." She dropped her hands. "I was twenty. And I was thrilled at his attentions. Even my parents respected him. I was going to have exactly the kind of life I'd been raised to believe every good girl wanted. He wanted children. Right away. Though it took several years for me to conceive. So long that I thought there was something wrong with me. By then I knew what my place was supposed to be. He wanted the properly bred, proper-looking wife and mother in his house. But he didn't really want *me*. Having my life managed by him didn't mean I was adored by him."

"I'm ten years older than you. Is that what you think I want? That any beautiful young woman would do? Dammit, Mel, if that's what I wanted, I could have had my pick of women long ago."

She glared at him and he sighed roughly. "That didn't sound right."

"No kidding."

"I don't want a trophy wife, Mel. We both have a chance, here. I want a marriage. With you."

She moved, dislodging the pillows, and pushed to her feet. "You don't love me, and I refuse to lose myself in that world all over again! I'm not strong enough, Luke, don't you see that?"

"*What* world?"

"*Your* world." She waved her hand, encompassing him. "You're a surgeon, too. I know how it is. I grew up in that world, and I married into that world. The family comes second to the patients, always."

"Mel—"

But she wasn't finished. "I'm not begrudging that. Truly. If it weren't for surgeons, Nicky wouldn't have lived as long as he did. But it's all the rest. The dinners. The benefits. The committees. I had a degree in foreign languages, but the only thing I was allowed to do with it was emcee a fund-raiser fashion show put on by a French designer!"

A bark of laughter escaped him. He wasn't even sure he'd be welcomed back at the clinic even if he *could* go back into the O.R. without puking. Sunquest's budget was tight enough without carrying a surgeon who couldn't cut it. "You're kidding me. I hate that stuff. Jason could quote you chapter and verse on just how bad at it I am. It's one of the reasons he wanted me out of the way. So I wouldn't screw up a fund-raiser that he has scheduled."

She whirled around, her eyes glistening. "Well, I hated it, too. But I did it all, Luke. I fit right in just the way my mother taught me. But none of it was compensation for a husband who only cared that I stayed

because of appearances. I was the mother of his child—
even though he couldn't even admit to loving Nicky—
and he didn't want his associates thinking he couldn't
keep his personal life under control.

"I won't try to keep you out of the babies' lives,
Luke. But I won't marry you. And I won't go with you
to Arizona."

"You want to stay here on this little island, hiding
out for fear that the past might repeat itself."

"It nearly finished me, Luke. Leaving behind everything that was familiar, even if it was slowly choking
the life out of me. My mother—" She pressed her lips
together for a moment. "I went to my mother and told
her I wanted to leave Jonathan, thinking that maybe
she'd understand. But I was a fool. She was sad about
Nicky's death, but she said I was just being ungrateful.
That I had a husband with a prestigious career and a
beautiful home. She said I was obviously unbalanced
because of Nicky and that I should turn around and go
right back to my husband. A husband who never once
shed a tear over losing our son; who never gave away
any of his feelings or his emotions. Everything was
always on his terms." Her voice was raw.

"You still love him."

She shook her head. "I stopped loving Jonathan
Deerfield the day he wanted me to have an abortion
because the prenatal tests showed Nicky wasn't perfect."

Luke closed his eyes, seeing the full circle of it all.
Deerfield had been the first surgeon to treat April.
That's how Mel had met Maisy. And she'd come to
Turnabout where she'd done a partial job of burying

her grief, only to meet *him*. When Mel had gotten pregnant, she'd avoided acknowledging it as long as possible so that if the results weren't perfect, she wouldn't
have to relive the kind of choice her ex-husband had
tried to force on her.

And now here they were.

Mel and Luke.

On opposite sides of a fence that she'd built, while
he had no idea how to tear it down.

He could force the issue when it came to their
babies. Paternal rights were alive and well and gaining
popularity by the day with the courts. But Luke refused
to go that route. Maybe it was pride, maybe it was
something else. He wanted Mel and their children, but
not by legal maneuvering.

Regardless of the past, he knew she wasn't the type
of woman she described. "You're wrong, you know,"
he said. "You are strong. Everything about you, what
you've lived through, what you've changed, proves it."

She was stronger than he was, when it came down
to it. Because he just kept avoiding the problem that
kept him awake at nights.

Her lips pressed together, her entire being seeming
to reject his words, and frustration coursed through
him.

"I don't care if you paint your face blue and twist
balloons for a living, if you attend one single dinner or
committee or benefit. The only one who thinks she's
got to force herself into some mold of your so-called
appropriate doctor's wife is you. I know half a dozen
women—wives—who could show you that mold
doesn't exist. Maybe it used to. Hell, it probably did.

But not anymore. And not with me. I want you to think about one thing, though. And think about it well, Mel, because it's the future of our babies that we're talking about. What are you really afraid of? Taking one more chance or letting go of the past?''

Then, before he did something really stupid, like tell her he loved her when it was so bloody damned clear that she did not love him, he strode from the cottage, the wooden screen door banging after him.

Chapter 16

"Hey, there." Mel poked her head in the room at the clinic that Hugo had outfitted for Maisy. "How are you feeling?"

Maisy, sitting up in the hospital bed that someone had managed to procure, shrugged. Her face was wan, her vibrant hair without its usual spark. "Like I've been pulled backward through a knothole. Plus Hugo's got me on some new thing to keep my blood pressure down."

Mel scooted the plastic side chair that was against the wall closer to the bed. "You never indicated that you weren't feeling well. Why didn't you say something?"

Maisy huffed. "You're a fine one to talk."

That was true enough. Mel sighed. "How long will the cast be on?"

"Weeks." Maisy's thin fingers plucked at the light

blanket covering her. "Everything okay at the inn? That couple from Alaska arrive okay?"

"Everything's fine." She'd checked on all the guests that day herself, except one. Mel wasn't prepared to face Luke just yet. She'd refused him; she didn't have the strength to do it again. If that meant avoiding him, then that's what she'd do. Cowardly or not, it was the only way she could get through the day. "Tomas met the new people at the dock this afternoon. They're all settled. Has Lily brought April by to see you yet today?"

"No. She…she had another episode last night. Hugo had to go over. He gave her a shot for the pain."

Mel's mouth dried. April had been doing so well, managing the pain with only an occasional pill. "Lily didn't tell me that."

"I didn't want her upsetting you and the babies." Maisy's eyes grew red. "She's needed her pills every day, Mel. The pain just gets worse. I can't bear for her to have more pain. I've just been a selfish old woman and enough is enough. I see that now."

Mel shook her head, pressing her forehead for a moment to Maisy's hand. "Oh, Maisy. You should have said something. Told me. Do I really seem so fragile to everyone? As if I can't take care of myself? You know how I feel about April. You could have told me."

Maisy cleared her throat and tsked. "Hardly fragile, chicken. Hardly that. But you do have a tendency to hold everything inside you."

Mel didn't know what to say to that.

"Chicken, you trust Luke. Don't you?"

Mel's lips parted. "Maisy, I—"

"Don't you?"

It wasn't Luke she didn't trust, but herself. After all, he hadn't let her down once since he'd returned to Turnabout only to discover she'd kept an enormous secret from him. "Yes. I trust him."

"And when it comes to April?"

Mel hesitated, immediately wondering where Maisy was heading. She easily remembered the day that April had fallen asleep in Luke's lap. "I don't believe he'd use her to glorify his own work."

"You think I should let her go to that clinic. To Sunquest. Let them examine her. Run their tests and God knows what else."

"Yes," Mel said gently. She rubbed her hand over her forehead, barely noticing that she was trembling. "Agreeing to an evaluation doesn't necessarily mean that April will have to have surgery again. Maybe she only needs a change in meds. Maybe there's something other than surgery."

"That's what Hugo's been saying. Man never shuts up. He tells me Dr. Frame considers Luke the best. Well, all right then. Go get the man. I want to see his face when I talk to him."

Mel scooted the chair back against the wall and headed back to the inn. It seemed no matter what she did, avoiding Luke was impossible.

When she got there, though, he wasn't in his cottage. Her heart jumped up in her throat and stayed there until she peered through the window and saw that his belongings were still inside—a shirt tossed over a chair, his boots lying on their sides on the floor.

"You're a lunatic, Melanie Summerville," she muttered, and turned back to the inn. Lunch was long over, and neither Tomas nor Leo, who was hobbling around with a cane even as he did his job making small repairs around the place, had seen him.

Luke wasn't at the clinic, and he wasn't at Maisy's Place. So where was he?

Their beach.

The thought had barely whispered into her mind when she slid into the golf cart and started driving down toward the beach.

He was there. Sitting on the sand, staring out at the jeweled glitter of the water.

Battling down her nerves, she climbed from the cart, slipped off her shoes and made her way across the powdery sand.

He didn't turn his head as she approached, but he obviously knew she was there, for he spoke as she neared. "Makes a person's life and all their problems seem small in comparison."

"Watching the ocean? Yes." Goodness knows she'd lost her painful thoughts in the mesmerizing magnificence of it all more than once. "What problems are you and the water working out?"

He looked at her.

She flushed. "Well. I, um, was looking for you."

He lifted his eyebrows.

"Maisy sent me to find you, actually. She wants to see you."

His lips twisted. "Of course. You wouldn't come of your own accord, would you."

She paused at that. But her assigned task waited.

"She wants to talk to you about April. She's willing to have her evaluated."

He absorbed that. "Jason'll be pleased."

"And you?"

"The girl needs treatment. Yeah. I'm pleased."

"You don't look it."

He rolled to his feet, the open lapels of his blue shirt rippling in the breeze. His chest was broad, hard and dusted with hair. She curled her fingers against the tingle that shivered across her palms.

His lips stretched into a smile that seemed macabre given the dark shadows in his eyes. "Better?"

"No. You haven't slept, have you? I can tell just by looking at you. You look—"

"What?"

"Terrible," she said on a faint sigh. "I'm sorry. I didn't want things to be like this."

He made a rough sound then put his hands on her shoulders. "What is it that you *do* want, Mel?"

There were shadows under his eyes, as well as in them, and she was distinctly aware that she was not necessarily the cause of them. Feeling impotent to change anything, she shook her head. "I don't know what you want me to say."

He exhaled slowly. "Why does it even matter to you what I want?"

"Of *course* it matters. Everything about you matters."

"But not enough to marry me." He let go of her shoulders and shoved his hands in his pockets. "Maisy's waiting, I assume."

Feeling unsteady and not liking it one bit, Mel nodded. He watched her for a moment longer, then turned and headed toward the cart parked on the sand.

She slowly followed, wondering why it felt as if something precious was slipping through her grasp.

Luke took the wheel and he drove the cart straight back to the clinic. He didn't speak. Neither did she. And when they arrived, she hurriedly climbed from the cart before he could do his usual thing of coming around and helping her from it as if she were made of crystal.

Maisy was awake and waiting when they stepped into the room. Hugo sat on the chair beside her, the cigar clenched between his teeth. The air seemed thick with tension.

"About time," Maisy said tartly when they stepped into the small room.

"Calm your jets, woman."

"Choke on your cigar."

Hugo glared at her. Maisy glared back.

Mel cleared her throat. "Maisy, I told Luke about April."

"Good. Then you can get right on it. I talked with Dr. Frame while you were lollygagging. Mel, you can go with Luke back to Arizona and take care of April."

"What?"

Maisy had the grace to appear contrite as she looked up at Mel. "If you're with April then she'll be all right. At least until I get out of this contraption and can join you."

Mel was excruciatingly aware of the steadying hand Luke had settled at the small of her back. "Why not wait until you're on your feet again and then make the trip together?''

''Because April's condition is worsening,'' Luke said quietly. ''Isn't it?''

Maisy glanced up at Luke. ''I can't wait until Hugo here gives me the clear to get on my feet again. Darned man seems to think I'm gonna keel over with a stroke or something—'' Her voice choked and she hauled in a breath.

''Easy, girl,'' Hugo muttered, ''or I'll call off this little tea party.''

Maisy's lips tightened. ''I can't send Lily with April—she has to take care of her little sister.'' Her voice was calmer. ''But I can send you, Mel. And I know what I'm asking, but—''

Mel wanted to weep for the impossible situation. ''Of course I'll go with April. You don't have to ask twice. I love her.''

''I know you do.'' Maisy looked at Luke. ''She visited every day we were at the hospital in San Francisco. She was there because Nicky was there, too, but she always took time to look in on us, on all the pediatric wing's patients for that matter. She was always kind that way.''

Kind. Mel watched Luke, afraid of what she'd see in his face. But his expression showed nothing at all. ''And you've already spoken with Jason,'' he said.

''He said to tell you he's sending the plane. It'll be here by nightfall.''

Mel started. ''So quickly?''

''Jason's not one for sitting on his thumbs,'' Luke

said flatly. "It's one of the reasons he's the best at what he does."

"And he says you're the best at what you do. That if anyone can help my granddaughter, it's you."

Luke's eyes narrowed. "He did."

Maisy nodded. "And I know April trusts you. She may not see, but she *sees*."

"And what do *you* see?" Luke asked, his voice low.

"I see you standing beside Mel," Maisy said after a moment. "So, I know that she's in the best hands. Yours and Mel's."

Luke didn't answer that. His jaw was tight and Mel felt nervousness bubble in her stomach as he looked at her. "Then I'd better grab my gear," he said simply before he strode from the room.

Maisy didn't look at Mel. "I know it's a huge favor, chicken."

Mel watched down the hall until she couldn't see Luke any longer. "Anything that helps April isn't too huge."

"She's still at Lily's. She's bringing April here in a little while. I haven't told them what I've decided."

"You're doing the right thing, Maisy," Hugo said gruffly. "April's going to be happy to do anything you say is best. She'll probably look on it as some great adventure. Now, I oughta make sure everybody stays off the road or that plane isn't going to have any place to land."

Maisy's gaze tracked Hugo's progress. When he was gone, she looked at Mel, all business. "You'd better go pack, too. Goodness only knows how long you'll be there with Luke."

"I'm going with April," Mel said quickly. "I won't be staying with Luke."

"Oh, don't talk nonsense, girl. Of course you'll stay with him. He's the father of those babies of yours. You think he's going to allow you to be anywhere other than with him?"

"Maisy, you know how I feel about—"

"About marriage and surgeons and losing yourself somewhere in the mix. I know, I know. Just give the man a chance, Mel. Give love one more chance."

"I don't love—"

"Bah." Maisy waved her hand. "Chicken, you are so in love with that man that even April could see it on your face. Now, go on. Get yourself ready. Tell Tomas he's in charge and that he'd better not mess up the reservations like he did that one time, or I'll have his hide. He should see if little Janie Vega can come in and help out with breakfasts like she did last year when I had the flu. George can manage the rest of the cooking like he usually does."

Still Mel hesitated. "I don't want to leave you, either, Maisy."

The other woman's expression softened. "I'm going to be fine, chicken. Hugo will see to that. He's a pain in my side, but he'll do that. I'll be fine. And so will you."

Mel's eyes burned. "It's only for a week or two," she reasoned, knowing it was only her own self that needed reasoning. "Probably. Then—"

"You can always come back here, Mel. You know that. But it's time to put the past to rest. Nicky's gone.

You loved him enough for both you and his father. But let him go. And look to the future. You all deserve it.''

Mel swallowed the knot in her throat and quickly hugged Maisy. The woman had been more of a mother to Mel in the years she'd known her than Mel's own mother. "I know, Maisy. I just can't chance raising my children in the same way that I was raised.''

Maisy cupped Mel's cheeks and clucked her tongue. "I've met your mama, Mel. Just one time in passing at the hospital in San Francisco, but it was enough. You're nothing like her and no amount of yammering will convince me otherwise. Trust yourself for once. You've been doing all right, but you won't even let yourself take credit for it. Now, go on with you. You've got some packing to do.''

Since there seemed nothing else to say, Mel left. Luke hadn't taken the cart with him and she drove back to Maisy's Place, her emotions spiraling.

She stopped by the inn to tell Tomas he was in charge and then went to her cottage. But once there, she could only stand in the center of the living room, not knowing where to start.

"Mel? Are you packed?''

She whirled around. Luke stood behind her. She hadn't even heard the squeak of the door, she'd been so lost in thought. "What?''

"Are you packed?'' His gaze took in the room. "Where's your suitcase?''

"I don't have one. I'll have to use a box or a plastic bag or something.'' She shook her head, feeling tears threaten again. Maybe it was hormones or maybe she was really as ridiculous as she feared. What kind of a nut cried over whether or not she had a suitcase? "When I came to Turnabout, I didn't have anything with me. Only what I'd stuffed in my purse. Some cash." She slid open the drawer next to the sofa and withdrew the photograph of her sweet son and the tuning fork. "And these."

He took the small frame and looked at the photo. "Why the tuning fork?"

"Nicky liked to play with it."

"When you said you walked away from it all, you weren't exaggerating." He handed her the frame. "Pull out whatever you want to take. Your clothes, anything else you've collected since you came to Turnabout. I'll go find you a suitcase."

"You don't need to keep taking care of me, Luke."

"Yeah," he said evenly, "I do. Because taking care of you is all I have left."

Chapter 17

"Is she settled?"

"Yes." Mel smoothed her hand over April's curls where they lay against a soft yellow pillowcase. "She was thrilled with the plane ride. But it exhausted her."

Luke nodded. He silently rounded the bed and pulled out the metal chart that hung on the side of a whitewashed wooden dresser. This private room that April had been settled in minutes after a car had whisked them from a small airfield to Sunquest looked far more like a lovely bedroom than a hospital room.

"I've assigned a private duty nurse for her," he said. Mel could hear the faint scratch of his pen as he made notations on the chart. "Denise Blankenship is young and extremely capable. I think April will like her. All of our kids do. She'll probably be here any minute now."

"Oh, but I—"

"I'm not saying you can't stay with April anytime you want. But you're not a nurse, Mel."

She subsided, knowing he was right. "Will she be with her all night? I wouldn't want April to wake alone."

"She'll be at the nurses' station."

"Then I'm going to stay here." She looked around the comfortably appointed room. "I can sleep in that chair."

He rubbed the bridge of his nose, looking weary and beautiful and completely removed. "You're six and a half months pregnant, Mel."

Her spine stiffened, though it was an effort considering that she felt fairly exhausted herself. Riding an emotional roller coaster had that effect. Pile on a couple hours on a small plane that could have doubled for an airborne emergency room, and she wanted only to sit down and put up her feet. "Yes," she said, smoothing her hand over the inordinately active babies. "I sort of noticed."

His lips tightened. "Fine. Suit yourself."

She frowned, put off balance by his seeming agreement. "That's all you have to say?"

"You're a grown woman, Mel. As you've ably argued, you can decide what is best for you." His gaze skipped over her. "You don't need me to tell you that your ankles are swollen. You already know. Feel better?"

It was foolish. "Yes."

His lips twisted. "I'll be in my office. The driver who met us at the airport took your stuff to my place. If you need anything, check with the nurses."

"Aren't you going home? You need some sleep, too."

"I'll go when you'll go with me." He went out the door. "Don't forget. You need something, you ask."

And just like that, she was alone in the silent room with the sleeping April.

Mel blinked. "Well." She rubbed her hands down her arms and adjusted the sheet covering April's thin shoulders. Then she maneuvered the chair around—it was far easier than she'd expected because there were casters hidden beneath the upholstered skirt—until it was closer to the bed. She sat down, kicked off her shoes and propped her feet on the end of April's bed. It wasn't the most comfortable she'd ever been, but it would do for now.

The babies bumped and rolled inside her and she smoothed her hand over them, willing them to be calm. If they were, then two out of three wouldn't be bad.

Luke went to his office after he left Mel and April. It seemed stale and musty inside, though, as if it hadn't been used in months. Considering how little time he'd been there since January, it was no wonder. And in those few days a week that he'd forced himself to attend to his work—if only to consult—he'd hardly been the model of organization. Jason should have fired him, he thought grimly. Only years of non-stop work had earned him a *lot* of vacation time. There was a pile of files covering one side of his rough-hewn desk. Covering the other side were stacks of correspondence. Notes from the other doctors on staff. Letters from doctors the world over regarding patients, invitations to speak, teach, attend.

He sighed and picked up one invitation in particular. Ivory parchment and sedate black ink.

"The prodigal son returns."

Luke dropped the invite back on the pile and glanced over at Jason. "Hardly prodigal," he said flatly. He rounded the desk and sat down. "You look like you just walked off a golf course." -

Jason, silver-haired and bronze-skinned, chuckled. "Lydia dragged me out for an evening round. Too hot to golf otherwise."

Luke eyed his boss. Jason Frame had been his mentor and his friend. "You hate golfing."

"Yeah, but my wife loves it," Jason countered. He entered the office and sat on the long butter-soft couch that had seen Luke through more nights than his own bed had. He stretched out his legs. "And I love my wife, so there you go. You look like hell. The vacation was supposed to do you some good, Luke."

Luke spread his fingers, staring at his hands. As long as he'd known Jason, Lydia had been by his side. Forty-one years of devotion, of support. "Do you have the Conroys appeased?"

Jason made an impatient sound. "Hell, son, you know that's not the only reason I kicked your tail out of here for a while. The Conroys are fine, and the fundraiser is on course. It took some doing to convince them that you hadn't trifled with their darling daughter's affections. But Belinda's already moved on to her next quarry and now we've very nearly got the rest of the funding we need for the new wing. Did you ever doubt it?''

''Doubt you?'' Luke smiled faintly and shook his head. ''No.''

''You're too busy doubting yourself. It's not going to get better until you get back in the O.R., Luke. You know that as well as I do. You get kicked off the horse, you climb back on.''

''If I'd stuck with horses, Jennifer Melendez would still be alive.''

Jason sat forward. ''How many cases have you treated, Luke? Too many to count. And you never lost one on your table.''

''Not until Jennifer.'' She'd been fourteen years old. The same age as Bethany when she'd died. Jennifer could have been her twin, with wavy black hair and snapping brown eyes. Bethany's death had been out of Luke's hands.

Jennifer's had not.

''The review board was conclusive. You did everything right.''

''But she still died, didn't she.'' Luke slammed his hand on the desk, pushing to his feet. ''I signed the papers on my grandfather's ranch one day and walked into that O.R. the next and killed that girl.''

''Dammit to hell, Luke. I know you weren't happy about selling the ranch. You were upset. But that didn't affect your performance. Jennifer Melendez had about a five percent chance of surviving no matter *what* you did or did not do in that O.R. You did everything humanly possible to prolong her life, even if only for a matter of weeks. I've seen you in action, Luke, too many times to worry that your concentration isn't exactly where it needs to be. On your patient. But even with you, sometimes skill isn't enough.''

"The surgery was successful but the patient died," Luke repeated the old humorless joke.

"That's pretty much it," Jason said flatly. "You've never been the kind of man who believed that your skills with the scalpel superseded a patient's will to live or die. You believed that it was the combination of the two that meant success.''

"So you sent me to Turnabout in January after it happened 'cause you knew there was no way I could turn my back on that little girl sleeping down the hall.''

"Well." Jason shrugged. "It took you longer than I figured it would. And I'd pretty much given up hope until I found out you headed back there again. You're the best surgeon Sunquest has, Luke. If April gets you back in the saddle, then we've two victories to celebrate.''

Luke knew, though, that it was the memory of Mel that had lured him back to Turnabout the second time. He'd spent six months trying to erase thoughts of her through every means possible—including Belinda Conroy's inventive charms. He'd been no more successful at forgetting Mel than he was at accepting what had happened in his O.R. It was only a matter of time before Jason had to cut him loose. A surgeon who couldn't operate was nothing but a liability.

"I had nothing to do with changing Maisy Fielding's mind about April," he said. "She did that all on her own.''

"Maybe. Maybe not. Who's to say what all conditions are present to make a person do one thing or another. The point is, April's here. We'll see if we can do anything about her situation, and go from there.''

''And if somebody's gotta scrub, you think it'll be me.'' Even though there were other perfectly able surgeons on staff, who had been picking up his slack for months now.

''From what I saw of April's history in Dr. Hugo's charts, I know that, even scared spitless, you're that child's best hope.''

Pain throbbed in his temples as Luke told Jason about April's previous treatment. ''What makes you think I can accomplish what a guy like Jonathan Deerfield couldn't?''

''Because Jonathan is a coldhearted son of a bitch,'' Mel's voice came from the doorway. ''And you're not.''

Luke stared.

Mel's dark gaze flickered over Jason, who'd risen. ''Hello, Dr. Frame. It's good to see you again,'' she greeted. ''I assume Maisy informed you that I was accompanying April?''

''Yes.'' His gaze was on her obviously pregnant form. ''She didn't mention anything about this, however. Congratulations.''

Luke caught the quick glance Mel sent his way. ''Thank you'' was all she said, though. She tucked her silky hair behind one ear. ''April's still sleeping. Denise is there. You were right, Luke. She's very nice. I...decided that it probably isn't necessary for me to stay in April's room.''

''Of course we've got accommodations here at Sunquest for family members," Jason said immediately. "You're all set up—"

"I'm sorry." Mel's cheeks were red. "Thank you for the offer, but I'll be staying with Luke."

Silence settled on the room. A portion of Luke's mind was aware of the considering look Jason sent from Mel to him. Mostly he was aware that, given a choice, Mel had chosen him.

"Well," Jason finally said. "That seems all taken care of then, so I'll get out of your hair and see you in the morning." He smiled at Mel as he passed her for the door. "Lydia will be delighted to see you, Mel, when she learns you're visiting." He patted her arm as he left.

Luke leaned back in his chair and looked at Mel. "How much did you hear?"

"Enough." Her eyes were soft and she slowly closed the office door before walking over to the desk. She did the same thing he had; ran her fingers over the pile of correspondence. "I wish you'd told me."

"So you could talk Maisy out of trusting me?"

She made a sound. "Of course not." The line on his desk buzzed, and she pressed her lips together.

He exhaled and grabbed the phone. "Trahern." His gaze didn't leave Mel as he listened for a moment. "Yeah. Five minutes." He dropped the phone on the cradle. "I've—"

"Got to go. I know. I recognize the drill. Go."

She recognized it and was probably already finding him wanting, he thought blackly. "I'll have a driver take you to my place. It's only ten minutes from here."

"No. I'll go when you go."

"Turning my words around on me, Mel?"

"Maybe." She eyed his couch. "That looks more comfortable than the chair in April's room. I'll just stretch out here and wait." To prove it, she glided past him, her arm brushing against his, and settled on the couch, turning on her side and tucking her arm beneath her head. Her hair flowed around her and her eyes looked like black opals. "Go on, then. Someone needs you."

"But not you."

"I'm here, aren't I?"

"Not by choice."

"There's always a choice," she whispered, her gaze following him to the door. "A lot of things happen that are out of our control. But how we deal with it? There's the choice."

"Grandfather 101."

"Maisy Fielding." Her lips curved faintly. "Graduate course."

Luke watched her for a long moment. Then he turned and went to deal with the nurse who needed help with an unruly patient.

Mel's eyes came open with a start. It only took a moment to remember where she was.

Sleeping on the couch in Luke's office.

Her gaze drifted over the painfully silent room. There was a clock on the credenza behind Luke's desk. An old-fashioned mantel clock. The kind that had to be wound with a key. It was undoubtedly the clock Luke had taken from his grandfather's ranch. Along with the desk, before he'd signed away the property.

The clock was silent and it struck her as inordinately sad. She sat up, pushing aside the soft butterscotch throw that had been covering her legs, and swung her bare feet to the floor. Someone had covered her. Had placed her shoes beside the couch where they'd be easily found.

Not someone.

Luke.

Ignoring the shoes, she walked over to the clock and studied it for a moment. She ran her fingertip along the gold circle framing the round glass plate, felt the invisible latch. The glass swung open. The key—oversize just as Luke had mentioned—sat beside it and she picked it up. She'd seen clocks like it before, of course. But never one that she knew to be handmade. Never one that had a small window indicating the month and day. She leaned closer, reading the faded gold engraving. The fifth of January.

Her throat closed and she sat down in Luke's big desk chair, closing the key in her fist. Luke had taken the clock from his grandfather's house. But he obviously hadn't wound it once, since.

"We're a pair, Luke Trahern," she whispered.

She wound the clock, set the time and, after some effort, figured out how to adjust the date, as well. Then she gently pushed the glass front closed. It snapped into place. The quiet, soothingly rhythmic ticking of the clock sounded throughout the silent office.

She set the key back in the same spot beside the clock and left the office.

She certainly didn't expect to find Luke in April's room. But not only was he there, he was sleeping.

He'd pulled up that same chair and propped his feet on the end of the bed, just the way she'd done.

Mel realized she'd never watched him sleep. His lashes were thick smudges against the bronzy olive cast of his face. His lips were more relaxed. Softer. Kissable.

She pressed her fingertips to her temples, willing away the jolting ache that warmed her insides and made her want to brush her mouth across his. She put April's bed between her and Luke, and sat in the other, smaller side chair.

"I thought you'd sleep until morning." Luke's eyes were heavy lidded, and impossibly intense as he watched her across the small mound of child sleeping on the bed.

She pressed her hand to her heart. "I didn't mean to disturb you."

"You've been disturbing me for months now."

Mel's gaze flicked to April. If she'd thought to find some protection from that quarter, she was sorely mistaken. The little girl's lips were parted, so deeply asleep she was very nearly snoring.

She moistened her lips. "You'll be starting her tests right away in the morning, I assume."

He gave a barely perceptible nod. The weight of his gaze was like a physical caress. She swallowed and cleared her throat. "And if you decide s-surgery is the way to—"

"I'm ready to go home," he said.

Her mouth dried. Her heart stuttered, then charged. She opened her mouth to speak but found she had no words.

The corners of his lips lifted and if she'd thought he looked dangerously sexy while dozing, it was nothing compared to the way he looked now. Like a languorous big cat that had spotted his quarry and was slowly circling it. "You do get silent at the most interesting times, Mel." He waited a beat. "Remember that night?"

As if she could forget.

"There was one thing we were both looking for."

Her paralyzed tongue finally broke loose. "Peace."

"Yeah." He pulled his legs from the bed and stood. "Only time I get close to that feeling is when I'm with you. Now I have one question before I go home and take you with me."

She rose, also, too agitated to sit. "What?"

"Which room are you gonna sleep in? The guest room? Or mine."

Chapter 18

In the shadowed light of the room, Luke watched Mel's face as he waited for her answer. Her lashes slowly lowered, and she caught her lip between her teeth.

"We've done everything backward."

It was hardly either response he might have expected.

She tucked her hair behind her ear, took a few steps along the bed, then hesitated. If she knew how she drove him mad, he'd never have a moment's freedom for the rest of his days. "How so?"

Another step took her to the end of the bed. She smoothed her hand over the swell of their babies. "We started here. And have gotten to know each other… some…after the fact."

"Nobody said it was the perfect situation. But I'm not complaining."

"No. You're not." Her slender hand drifted along the hospital-cornered bedding. "I'm sorry I didn't contact you right away. It was wrong, cowardly, of me."

"Mel, it's over. We're here, now."

She moistened her lips. Took another inching step around the bed. "Yes, but I think it's only fair... right...that I should tell you that, had we not done things backward, had you and I gotten to know each other some, properly, you know—"

"Get to the point, Mel."

"I'd still choose you to be the father of my children." She stopped in front of him.

She was killing him. Slowly but surely, degree by painful degree. "Which room, Mel."

"Yours."

He let out a long breath. Slid his hand down her arm and caught her hand in his. He stopped at the nurses' station to let Denise know they were leaving. Then, out of necessity, they stopped by his office so he could retrieve the keys to his car, which had been parked in the covered lot since he'd been banished by Jason. They were in the drawer inside his credenza. He bent over, closed his hands on the keys and straightened.

Then he noticed the soft tick-tick-tick. He looked at Mel. "You set the clock."

"It seemed a shame to leave it there. It was all alone, stuck in the past." Her cheeks colored. "You probably think that sounds ridiculous."

"I think it sounds familiar."

She finally nodded, set her shoulders and held out her hand. "Can we go, now?"

He took her hand and led her from the office, out of

the building and into the quiet night. Their footsteps sounded loud across the pavement to his car. "The city lights do go on forever, don't they," she murmured, looking out beyond the edges of Sunquest. "What kind of cactus is that? The one with the arms?"

"Saguaro."

"They appear to be standing guard."

Luke stopped and looked where she was focusing. Sunquest was slightly higher in elevation, giving the impression of surveying the valley below. Against the glow of distant lights, the cacti nearby stood tall, proud, the way they had for decades. "They do," he agreed. It had been a long time since he'd bothered to appreciate the stark, distinct beauty the desert had to offer. And while it *was* beautiful, it was steadily creeping toward dawn.

He steered her toward his car, and she went willingly. The drive, ten minutes on any other day, was made in seven. Later, when there was more time, he'd slow down, giving her time to absorb the scenic setting. He punched the button and drove straight into the garage the moment the doors swung wide enough and parked next to the '69.

The inner door from the garage led through the laundry room. The light went on automatically when they entered.

"Nice setup," Mel said, blinking against the sudden light. "There's as much room in here as there was in my house growing—"

He pulled her close and kissed her.

"—up," she finished faintly when he lifted his head a long while later. Her breath was unsteady, her hair tumbled, her dress already falling from her beautiful shoulders.

He considered it fair, given the state she'd had him in for months.

"This isn't your room, though."

He smiled slowly. He took her hand and led her through the house. There was a vase of fresh flowers on the dining room table. Lydia Frame, he thought. She'd be the only one to think of that particular touch, and she and Jason were the only ones Luke had given a key to while he'd been gone.

His room was on the far side. It took up the entire east side of the house, to be exact. It had a wall of windows that overlooked the city at night and welcomed the sun at dawn. "This one is," he said gruffly, and tugged Mel back into his arms.

The land surrounding his house went far and wide. Luke had never considered it before, but he was grateful then, for the complete privacy, as he stood with Mel in front of those windows, in the wash of moonlight, and slowly unwrapped her. Like a gift. Contents fragile, precious and incredibly beautiful.

"Your dresses always have so many buttons," he murmured, finishing the job he'd begun in the laundry room. "I've dreamed about your buttons. Undoing them." He slid the loosened bodice from her shoulders. It fell all the way to the carpet, pooling around her feet. Next went her bra, and her breasts, fuller and crested with velvety nubs taunted the palms of his hand, tempted his lips. He slid his hands over them, heard her breathe in sharply when he couldn't help but tarry there before running his touch over the warm, taut heat of her abdomen.

"H-hardly the pair I wore in January," she whispered, when he slid his fingers under her panties and drew them inexorably down her thighs.

He wondered if it was a woman thing. She was carrying twins. Wearing maternity clothes. Did she think he expected bikini panties? He was more interested in getting her naked. Fast. "You're beautiful." He rose, letting his eyes take his fill. "Do you doubt it?"

"I'm huge." Her words ended on a squeak when he tore off his shirt.

He felt her gaze rove over him. "You're carrying my children. You think that isn't appealing to me? Physically?" He saw her struggle, instinctively knew the cause of it and damned the man who had put insecurities into her lovely head. "We don't need a threesome," he said evenly. "It's only you and me, here, Mel. And I like what I see just fine." He popped open his strained fly. "Obviously."

Her lips parted, her gaze dropping. Staring. And he felt a faint laugh strangle in his throat.

"Well," she said huskily, "at least I'm not the only one who's huge."

He laughed, groaned, cursed, when her touch, too fleeting, too maddening, grazed him. "Wait. Can you do this?"

She made a soft sound. "You're the doctor."

"I'm not *your* doctor."

She touched him again. "Hugo gave the 'all clear,'" she whispered. "Before we left Turnabout."

Luke silently blessed Hugo. "The bed," he muttered. "Let's be novel. Try a bed finally." More specifically, *his* bed.

Graceful, womanhood personified, she stepped out of the clothing piled around her feet and turned to the bed.

Even that small distance between them was too much. He caught up to her, sliding his arm around her, cupping her breast, kissing the curve of her shoulder. Tall enough to fit him. His other hand smoothed over her belly, brushed through the downy triangle between her thighs. He could feel her trembling. Or maybe that was him. She was so responsive, so magical. A sound rose in her throat, that same sound, that hum of hers that had lived in his mind for more than six months now.

Her hands caught his, stilling him. "Not again," she whispered hoarsely, turning in his arms. "I want you with me this time." Her mouth sought his, her breath warm, sweet, arousing. Her hand reached for him, encircled him.

He groaned, and pulled her down onto the bed, settling her beside him. He'd let her set the pace. Go as slow as she wanted, as slow as she needed.

Mel couldn't touch enough of him, couldn't get enough. "I've heard about women having, heightened, uh—"

"Libidos," he provided, looking thoroughly content at the notion.

"Yes, but I never really had that trouble before you." Mel dragged his hands back to her breasts, nearly whimpering with delight, relief, want. "It's embarrassing," she whispered, "but I look at you and

I…want you.'' She sucked in her breath, then sighed out a moan when he plumped her breasts together. Tasted one, then the other. Her fingers slid through his hair. Her legs moved restlessly.

''Does it seem like I'm complaining?'' He guided her thigh over his hip and slowly thrust against her, sliding through her slick folds, not entering, but nearly blinding her with sensation anyway.

She sighed his name and pressed her mouth against his throat, tasting his pulse, his skin. She arched against him, twined her leg higher, but even then it wasn't enough, and with an impatient sound that shocked her, she pushed him back on the wide bed and slid over him, taking him.

He shuddered and groaned, bowed upward until they were breast to breast. Then he kissed her, and she felt him grow even harder inside her as she melted over him. His hands swept down her back, caught her hips, pulled her tight. ''One of these days,'' he growled, ''I'm going to get the top.'' He thrust slowly, deeply.

Her breath stuttered, pleasure spiking so fiercely she gasped. ''Are you complaining *now?*''

''No,'' his voice was rough. ''Only promising that when I do, I'm going to take my time.''

Her breathless laugh was cut to the quick when he kissed her and the coiling pleasure inside her unfurled in that blaze of ecstasy that only he could create. And in the dim reaches of her mind, as pleasure racked through them both, tearing her apart only to put her back together again more complete than ever before, she was aware of his arms holding her safe, her name on his lips.

* * *

Luke woke to the smell of coffee and the sight of Mel silhouetted against the golden dawn. She wore one of his shirts and the rising sunlight shone through the white fabric. "No wonder cultures as old as time have worshipped feminine images," he said.

She turned when he spoke. "Because we bring male images coffee in bed?"

His laughter was short. He threw back the sheets and climbed from the bed, heading toward her, ignoring the mug of coffee sitting on the nightstand. "It's not the coffee that's spurring me on at the moment."

Her smile was half shy, half lazy satisfaction. "I think, somewhere along the way in that very bed over there, you said we should get to Sunquest first thing this morning."

He swept her up in his arms, laughing softly when she gasped and insisted he put her right back down.

He did. Inside the shower. Which they shared.

And Luke took his time.

Chapter 19

Once April's tests were underway at the clinic, Mel was surprised at how quickly the time passed. She called Maisy around lunchtime, and April chattered for a few minutes before handing the phone over to Mel and tucking her head into her pillow, sleepy yet again. Mel had barely finished talking to Maisy herself when Denise came into the room bearing a wheelchair. Luke followed on her heels.

Mel swallowed, feeling heat in her cheeks. She hadn't seen him since that morning. Then he'd been wearing jeans and a Diamondbacks T-shirt. Now, he wore soft green scrubs that only defined his impressive body even more. When he leaned over to lift April's slight weight into the wheelchair, she found herself actually staring at his behind, completely inappropriate and thoroughly lascivious thoughts circling her mind.

Denise caught the direction of her gaze and grinned sympathetically.

Mel flushed even harder. Then Luke straightened, caught Mel's eye and heat streaked through more than her face. "We're going to do her MRI," he said. "Do you want to come, or wait here?"

"I'll come with you."

April grabbed Mel's hand. "What's an MRI? Is it gonna hurt?"

"Not a bit," Mel assured.

They headed down the hall and Luke explained what April could expect.

"Too bad we don't have an open MRI," Denise said beside her. "I know Dr. Frame has been trying to get the funding for it. As it is now, if patients have any sort of claustrophobia, we have to send them down to Phoenix."

April had let go of Mel's hand and was practicing wheeling the chair herself. Luke let her, only adjusting now and then to keep her from running right into the walls. "There's a new wing being built, I understand."

"A pediatric wing. Right now, we have to mainstream peds in with the adults. Dr. Trahern doesn't advertise it, but he was the one who spearheaded the effort. He's a special man. But I don't suppose I need to tell you that."

"Mel—" Luke looked back at her "—you can wait in there. You'll be able to see everything, and talk to April, as well." He gestured to a glass door and headed April through another set of double doors.

Denise pushed open the door and went inside, holding it for Mel. "We're all glad that Dr. Trahern came back,'' she said, as they watched Luke and April enter the room on the other side of the thick glass panels. ''He's one of a kind.''

''He's been spending a lot of time with April,'' Mel murmured. ''He got to know her and her grandmother on Turnabout—during his vacation, otherwise I'm sure he'd…'' Her words trailed off. She didn't know how to put it. Luke was spending much more time with April than was usual.

But Denise didn't seem to notice anything amiss. ''He's obviously fond of her,'' she agreed. ''But he's this way with all of his patients. Definitely not one of those types that sails into the O.R. at the last minute, seeing only the sterile field to apply his skills, and none of the individual beyond the drape.'' She laughed slightly, flushing. ''And yes, I'll admit, I'm one of the rest of the hoards around here who are crazy for the man. And not just 'cause he has a world-class hiney in his scrubs.'' She grinned, too engaging for anyone to take offense.

''If you're through admiring the scenery,'' the technician sitting at a complicated console spoke, ''maybe we could get on with this?''

Denise giggled and left the room, going into the other room to sit beside April, who was now lying on the narrow table that would slowly move into the machine. She'd sit with April during the test. Mel would have, but given her pregnancy, Luke had already cautioned her against it.

She drew in a deep breath, not entirely sure what kind of results for which to pray—that April's tumor would be deemed operable, or that they'd choose to treat it by some other means. Luke left the room and joined the technician at the console. And the test began.

And so it went.

During the day, Mel stayed at Sunquest, keeping April's flagging spirits occupied as she underwent test after test so Luke and his associates could determine their best course of action, finding herself the center of a good deal of attention by the nurses, and hearing again and again how well liked Luke was. During the night, she rested in Luke's arms. On the third night, she accused him of leaving the clinic before ten o'clock only because of her. He grinned, and asked if she was complaining.

Since she was presently enjoying the fruits of his labors, she assured him that she most definitely was not.

But underneath it all, Mel was excruciatingly aware of Luke's increasing tension and his flat refusal to discuss the matter when she broached the subject.

On Friday, she saw Dr. Frame for the first time since their arrival at Sunquest. He had stopped in, his wife with him, to visit April and drop off the gift of a stuffed animal that had a tape player built into its stomach, along with several tapes of children's stories. April was delighted and promptly began experimenting with the tapes and the headphones that were also provided.

Lydia Frame hung back in the room when her husband headed for his office, exclaiming over how well Mel looked. "I hope you've had a chance to find an appropriate dress for the benefit tomorrow night what with all the time you've spent here."

Mel felt her neck tighten warningly. "Well, I wasn't really—"

"Darling, you *have* to go. Luke is receiving an award from the governor. Hasn't he told you?"

Since it was obvious to them both that Mel knew nothing, she shook her head. Lydia chattered on about the distinguished award for outstanding service in the community. "Luke hates all that fuss, of course. Doesn't seem to realize the ripple effect he has on those around him. At first we thought he wouldn't be back from his vacation for the benefit, but then when you both returned, I juggled things around so he could receive the award that night. I know someone in the Governor's office."

"Mrs. Frame—"

"Oh, darling, Lydia. Please. Mrs. Frame makes me sound positively ancient." She smiled, a friendly, thoroughly comfortable middle-aged woman with an avid passion for golf. A passion only slightly surpassed by her interest in meddling, Mel suspected.

"Lydia," she began again, "whether or not Luke attends really has nothing to do with me."

Lydia blinked. "But...you're his fiancée."

"Did he tell you that?"

"Well, no, but I assumed...well, darling you are pregnant." She waved her hand, her expression falling. "I'm sorry. That's so old-fashioned of me, I know. People have babies all the time today without marriage. I just thought Luke would want—"

"He does. Don't think less of Luke, Lydia. I'm the one who's been...hesitant." It seemed a puny word.

"Hesitant over marrying Luke Trahern?" Lydia's

eyebrows skyrocketed. "Darling, he's probably the most elusive, eligible bachelor in this state. Whether you intended to or not, you've landed yourself quite a catch."

Mel felt her facial muscles freezing. The words were eerily similar to what her mother had said when she'd told her parents that Jonathan had proposed.

"All of that is only so much nonsense, of course," Lydia continued. "The only thing that matters is how you both feel. And Luke looks at you the same way my Jason looked at me way back when." She laughed. "Still does, now and then, come to think of it. See what you can do to drag his ornery hide to the benefit. It may not be important to Luke to receive thanks, but sometimes it is important for those who need to express it to have an opportunity to do so."

Mel felt panicked at the very thought of it. "I don't have a dress," she said, seizing on the very excuse that Lydia had already provided.

Lydia waved her hand. "Nonsense. We'll go shopping. Tomorrow morning. I'll pick you up at ten. We'll hit the shops and be done in a few hours, and you can get back to see this little doll-baby here." Before Mel had a chance to argue, she lifted April's earphone and told her goodbye, and strode out the door.

"I like her," April announced after Lydia's departure. "She has a nice laugh."

"Yes, she does," Mel agreed. Lydia's laughter was completely without falseness. And it very nearly disguised the steamroller she wielded.

"Are you gonna go to that thing she was talking about?"

"I don't know." Luke hadn't asked her to accompany him to the benefit. She wasn't sure how she'd react if he did.

"I miss Grammy."

Mel ruffled April's curls. "I know, pumpkin. Why don't we call her right now and you can talk?"

April nodded and Mel immediately reached for the phone, putting through the call. April's mood brightened considerably, and Mel whispered that she would come back in a while after the two had a chance to chatter to their heart's content.

In the hall, she nearly ran right into Luke. He caught her arms in his, steadying her. "Hey. You look like you're in a hurry somewhere."

Thoughts of special fund-raising benefits that he wanted to avoid—at least with her—dissipated the moment his thumbs rubbed over her shoulders. She swallowed, feeling her cheeks warm. "No hurry," she managed. "April's talking to Maisy on the phone."

The corners of his lips tilted slightly. His thumbs continued rubbing. In a slow circle across her arm, up over the curve of her shoulder. He was doing it deliberately, she knew. The dark gleam in his eyes told her so. She could hardly breathe. She moistened her lips.

The rattle of a cart broke through the heady spell he cast and Mel practically jumped back a half foot when it came into view, a white-haired volunteer wielding the heavy book cart. She passed by them with a smile.

Mel crossed her arms, avoiding the amusement in Luke's expression. "Saved by the books," he murmured. Then he drew his finger down her cheek and his amusement died. "Actually, I need to talk to Maisy, myself."

Mel went still. "You've made your decision about April."

He didn't deny it.

"She needs the surgery."

"I've already told Hugo," he said instead of answering. "He thinks Maisy is up to making the trip here."

"Right away?"

"This weekend would be good."

He didn't need to elaborate. Mel had known all along that he would probably act very quickly once a plan of treatment was determined. "When do you want to schedule it?"

"Monday morning."

"Maisy will want to tell April herself."

"I know."

Mel glanced up and down the corridor that was, once again, mercifully empty. "Mrs. Frame told me about the award you're getting at the benefit tomorrow night."

"Lydia has a really big mouth."

"Why hide it?"

"Why advertise it?" He grimaced. "We're not going, anyway."

"Why not?"

He just looked at her.

"Okay, so I said I hated those kinds of events. But this is important. They want to honor you, Luke." It wasn't Luke seizing an opportunity to bandy about his greatness. Maybe it was splitting hairs, but Mel saw a distinct difference. "What's so wrong with that?"

He pinched the bridge of his nose between his fingers. "Because I don't deserve it," he gritted. He dropped his hand. "Now, go back in there and get off your feet. I'll have somebody drive you home later today. Once Maisy gets here, there will be no reason for you to spend every minute with April."

He didn't wait for Mel to protest. He simply turned and strode off down the hall. She wanted to go after him, but he disappeared into another patient's room.

Sighing, she slowly turned back to April's room.

"Grammy wants to talk to you." She held out the phone to Mel.

"Well," Maisy said as soon as Mel said hello. "Are you two still dancing around each other, instead of with each other?"

Mel flushed. But how could she deny it? She and Luke might have found complete accord in the bedroom. But outside of it, she wasn't anywhere near as confident. "Nice to hear your voice, too," she said instead.

Mel didn't see Luke again that afternoon. He was as good as his word though when it came to Maisy. She arrived shortly after dinnertime, much to April's delight. Someone even moved another bed into April's room so that Maisy could sleep there at night. Mel knew it had to have been Luke. The bed also gave Maisy a comfortable way of coddling her broken leg. She also knew he hadn't made the offer so that Mel could stay with April around the clock. What had he said before they'd left Turnabout?

Taking care of you is all I have left.

So when a young man stopped by April's room, announcing that he was there to take Mel back to Luke's, she went without debate. She spent the rest of the evening wandering through his spacious home. She fixed dinner, aware of the faint hope inside her that he would appear to join her. But he didn't. She showered in his shower, wrapped herself in his robe and propped herself in the center of his bed.

And wondered what she was doing with her life and whether she was destined to spend it, yet again, with a man who couldn't share his emotions with her.

Only her heart knew what her head refused to recognize. That Luke actually *possessed* emotions, while Jonathan had not. Jonathan had never had any family he'd tried to live up to. His mother had died after Mel had married him, but she'd lived in Florida and Jonathan's schedule had been full. Mel had flown to Florida alone, attending the funeral of a woman she'd never met. Nor had Jonathan ever torn himself up over a patient. And if he'd ever grieved over Nicky, he'd never grieved with Mel.

She'd tried. So many times, she'd tried to reach Jonathan. After one too many puzzled looks, one too many suggestions that she go shopping or go to a spa, she'd finally realized that Jonathan just hadn't possessed any kind of emotional depth. Or at least, the depth that she'd needed. And she'd stopped trying.

And what are you doing to reach Luke? The small,

silent voice inside Mel haunted her as she lay sideways on the bed and hugged his pillow to her cheek.

Despite finally opening up about her marriage and her son, was she still keeping Luke at bay just as surely as he was her? Is that why he hadn't explained about the poor patient he'd lost even after he'd realized she'd overheard him and Jason discussing her? Why he'd kept silent about the benefit? The award?

She was sharing his bed. His house.

Her abdomen shifted and she smoothed her hand over the restless babies.

She was sharing his children.

And she was glad. If nothing else, Mel knew that she was glad that Luke had found her that night on the beach.

Sleep continued to elude her, and she finally reached for the cordless phone on his nightstand. It wasn't particularly late. She called Maisy to check on April, who'd eaten only a little for dinner and was sleeping again, under the effects of the powerful pain medication she'd been administered. Before she'd gone to sleep, Maisy had told April that she was going to have surgery on Monday morning. In typical April fashion, she'd accepted the decision with a barrage of questions that Luke had come in and patiently answered.

Mel had barely disconnected the call when the phone rang in her hand, and she was so startled, she answered it. It was Lydia, reminding her that she'd be by to pick her up at ten the next morning.

Though she knew it would be smarter to beg off, she surprised herself by not doing so.

For some reason, that small action was enough to

dissipate some of the fog that clouded her thoughts. And when she settled again in Luke's bed, tugging his pillow against her cheek, she finally slept.

It was completely dark when she awoke later. The soft lamp she'd left turned on had been turned off. But she didn't need to sweep her arm across the wide expanse of bed beside her to know that Luke wasn't there.

She tilted her head, listening, but all she heard were the now-familiar sounds of the silent house. The low hum of the central air-conditioning. The occasional call of an owl outside the windows. Maybe Luke had come and gone.

She lay there, fully awake now, feeling the babies bump and roll inside her, and with a huff of impatience, she climbed out of bed. She was beginning to have fantasies of a night slept all the way through without needing to visit the bathroom every few hours.

Not that Luke's bathroom was any hardship. It, alone, was larger than the bedroom she'd had at the cottage at Maisy's Place. Rather than the ornate gold and marble fussiness she'd been used to from her parents' house and then her husband's house, however, Luke's was warm, streamlined. Had she had an opportunity to choose fixtures, fittings, colors herself, she wouldn't change a thing. It was made for comfort, from the massive whirlpool tub to the stone-floored separate shower.

She dragged her attention from the shower and looked in the mirror, to see if she was actually drooling. Assured she was not, she flipped off the light and padded back through the bedroom.

A particularly hard little kick under her ribs made

her wince, and she rubbed her hand over her expanding belly. "Come on, guys, give your mom a break, okay?" The twins just kept flip-flopping, and Mel knew there was no hope of getting back to sleep just yet.

She went into the kitchen, and was perched on the bar stool at the mottled black-and-brown granite countertop, forcing down a glass of milk, when she heard a muffled sound.

Relief swept through her. Luke hadn't gone back to Sunquest after all. She followed the sound through the laundry room, to the garage.

And he was there, all right. She could see him around the edge of his sleek BMW. He was sitting on an overturned five-gallon drum, his dark head bent over whatever piece of his '69 he was currently coaxing back into life. "I thought I heard you," she said, and stepped down into the garage, rounding the cars. The floor was cement and warm beneath her bare feet. "I'm glad you came home."

He didn't look up.

She stepped closer and barely refrained from touching his hunched shoulder, running her fingers through the silky weight of his thick hair. "Luke, I know you're irritated with me about the benefit tomorrow night, but I—" Her gaze drifted past his body to the greasy engine part sitting on a spread of newspapers between his feet. Only it wasn't just covered in grease. It gleamed, wet and shiny.

She swallowed, dismay washing through her as her gaze slowly slid from the part to the hand he held oddly, stiffly, over it.

A hand covered in blood. She sucked in a harsh breath. All thoughts of a logical, sensible discussion about their future went flying right out the window.

"I think—" his voice was emotionless "—I might have cut myself."

"Might?" Her voice went up half an octave. "Are you kidding me? You're bleeding all over the floor! You're supposed to cut open other people. Not yourself."

His lips twisted and his eyes went dark. "Maybe this way is safer."

Chapter 20

Safer.

Right before Mel's eyes, blood flowed from a deep gash on the palm of his hand down his fingers. It gathered at the end of his middle finger, pooled, formed a fat drop and fell to the darkening puddle soaking into the newsprint. "Don't be ridiculous," she said as she ran to the built-in cupboards lining one wall. They were filled with tools, all things macho, as she'd teased him just the other day. She grabbed the roll of paper towels, uncaring that she'd dislodged a row of tools that clattered to the floor. She hurried back to him, yanking off a hank that she crumpled into a ball and pressed against his palm. "Hold that," her voice shook.

He sighed, slowly curling his fingers. "Don't upset yourself. Or the babies. It's not as bad as it looks."

She tore off another long strip, wrapping it around his entire fist. "Sure, not bad at all," she agreed hoarsely. "I just come out to the garage to find you bleeding to death all over the garage floor." She swiped her eyes when her vision blurred. "You need stitches."

His dark blue gaze drifted over her and she realized she was still only wearing her short blue nightgown. With an oath, she ran back into the house, pulling off the nightie and dragging a denim dress over her head. She pushed her feet into her sandals, grabbed her purse and darted back to the garage.

The paper towels were soaked through. "God," she cried. "You're a surgeon, Luke, what were you thinking?" She pulled the towels away, replaced them with more, wrapped his hand again. "Come on. We have to get you help."

"I *was* a surgeon," he said flatly.

She was looking around for his car keys. "Don't say that. It's a cut. You'll get stitches. You'll be fine." She prayed. Her own father had turned to academics when he'd broken his hand in a skiing accident because the fine mobility had been irreparably damaged. "Dammit, where are your keys?" She finally saw them still in the ignition. "Luke, come on. I'll drive. Sunquest is closest, right?" She rounded the car, opening the passenger door, tossing her purse inside.

Luke still hadn't moved.

Her heart was in her throat. She went back over to him and tucked her hands beneath his arm. "Come on."

He yanked out of her hold, his expression suddenly angry. "It's just a cut, Mel. Leave it alone. Leave me alone."

She blinked, stared. "Like you left *me* alone? Pushing and poking and prodding until you know everything that's in my head, my heart." She huffed impatiently, yanking more towels off the spool, tucking them around the last batch that was already starting to redden.

"I don't know what's in your heart."

"Love, you stubborn fool. Love!" She pulled at his other arm. "Now would you please come on! How do you think you're going to be able to help April if half your hand is missing 'cause you cut it off fixing some bloody carburetor!"

"I didn't cut off my hand." He rose but didn't take any steps away from the '69. "And it doesn't matter anyway, because my career has been shot since January!"

"This is about that patient of yours who died, isn't it. Because you're blaming yourself."

"What do you know about it, other than what you overheard that night from Jason?"

"I know plenty," she said evenly. "Though, goodness knows it hasn't come from you. Honestly, Luke, what do you think your staff talks about all day long but everybody else's business, particularly the exalted surgeons? You think I haven't heard, chapter and verse, about that poor girl you tried to save? Or about the hundreds that you *have?*"

"It's not Jennifer Melendez." His voice was tight. "It's the fact that I can't pick up a goddamned scalpel without wanting to puke. The fact that I can't sleep at night for seeing patient after patient on my table, only they're not alive and breathing—they're corpses, cold and beyond breath, expressions etched in eternity that damn me for my failures. And it only gets worse every day that goes on.''

She swallowed the sudden knot of tears that seemed large enough to choke her. She touched his chest. Felt the unsteady pulse of his heart against her palm. She'd wanted emotion. Only now it was enough to break her heart. ''You're only a man, Luke. With an incredible talent. And there is a little girl named April who trusts you to take care of her. It's not the rest of your staff, the other surgeons, not even Dr. Frame who convinced Maisy to take another chance. It was *you*.''

''I hardly talked to her about it!''

''You didn't have to. Maisy trusts you, Luke. April trusts you, and so do I. But unless we get your hand taken care of the point will be moot, because you won't be in any shape to do *anything!*''

''You haven't been listening to me,'' he said slowly, distinctly. ''My hand is not the problem. My head is.''

''Then shut off your head and follow your heart,'' Mel said huskily. ''That's the only reason I'm here with you. Because if I listened to my head, I'd have run far and fast the second you put your leather coat over my shoulders that night on the beach. Instead, I looked up at you, and all the kindness that is inside you, and…here we are.''

''Mel—''

''You sleep fine when you're with me,'' she whispered. ''I know, because sometimes, I'll lie there awake with these two dancing a midnight merengue inside me, and watch you sleep.''

"It's the only time I sleep fine," he said flatly. "With you."

"Well." She blinked. "I'm not going anywhere." The pink seeping through his paper towels was darkening. "Now, could we please go and have your hand taken care of? Because, you know, I've got to drive you, and I'll tell you here and now that despite being a surgeon's daughter, I never really enjoyed the sight of blood."

He snatched up the paper towels, bunching more around his hand. "Dammit, I'll drive."

"My name is Melanie," she said huskily, slipping into the driver's seat before he could. "Not 'dammit.'"

He rounded the car and climbed in. Mel reached over him, tugging his seat belt into place. Her forehead brushed his chin and she looked up into his dark eyes. "I love you, Luke," she whispered. "We'll get through this all, okay? April's surgery. The babies. Just don't shut me out. Because I can take just about anything but that."

A muscle in his jaw flexed. He caught her head with his uninjured hand and pressed his lips to hers for a long, aching moment. "Just tell me one thing," he said when their lips finally parted.

"Anything."

"You *do* have a legal driver's license, don't you? You were on Turnabout a long time."

She breathed out, groaning. Started the car, and whipped it out of the garage and down the winding road, heading straight to Sunquest. "I'm born and bred Californian," she said. "On my sixteenth birthday, my parents gave me a cute little Benz."

''That's not an answer,'' he muttered, bracing his good hand against the dash as she rocketed down the road and pulled up in front of the clinic in less time than he'd ever made it.

In the end, it turned out that Luke's hand wasn't as badly slashed as Mel had feared. It took stitches, certainly. But he hadn't damaged any tendons or nerves. After he was stitched up, bandaged, and shot full of antibiotic, it was well past midnight. By unspoken agreement, they went by to look in on April. Luke checked her chart. Mel pulled up her covers.

Maisy, leg propped on a mountain of pillows, slept soundly.

They drove home, Mel at the wheel again after proving that she did possess a license after all. Instead of tumbling exhausted into bed, however, they both seemed wakeful. Mel finally opened the glass doors leading out to the stone terrace that led down to the pool. ''Come on.''

She selected one of the chaise longues that was positioned to look out over the glowing lights of the city. ''Sit there.''

He eyed her but sat. She kicked off her sandals and sat down in front of him, pulling his hands around to rest with hers on the bulge of her stomach, careful of the thick bandage cushioning his injured hand. ''There,'' she murmured. ''Still hot outside, but bearable. And it's sort of like looking out at the ocean.''

''An ocean of light.''

''Are you making fun of me?''

''Not in this lifetime.''

She smiled faintly and rested her head back against

his chest, her temple right beside his chin in the spot that seemed made for her. But her smile faded as the worry bottled inside her crept back to the surface. "You didn't deliberately cut yourself, did you?"

He exhaled roughly. "No. I'm not that self-destructive, thanks."

She believed him. "Good. I'm glad."

"If I'd wanted to immobilize my hands, I'd have done a better job of it," he said evenly, "instead of just bleeding a mess over the carburetor that's going to have to be cleaned all over again now."

She closed her eyes, an unwilling smile tugging at her lips. "You're worried about the car part."

"Man and his engine, Mel. Serious stuff."

She watched a pinpoint of light moving across the inky sky. Wondered if it was a shooting star. Figured it was more likely an airplane. Phoenix had an incredibly busy airport. "How'd you end up working at Sunquest, anyway?"

"You're as full of questions as April."

"Well, I think that if I ask a dozen, you might conceivably respond to fifty percent."

She felt the long breath he drew in and let out. "I was on staff in Cheyenne," he said eventually. "I had a young patient that everybody else had written off as untreatable. But I'd read about Sunquest, about Jason's progressive efforts in treating neurological conditions. I contacted him."

"And the patient?"

Luke leaned his head back against the soft cushion. "I got a wedding invitation from her a few years ago."

"Did you go?"

"No."

"Why not?"

He thought back. "Wall-to-wall surgeries," he finally said. "I sent a gift."

She laughed softly. "I think you'd already given the bride the gift that mattered."

"Anyway, that's how I met Jason. That was nearly ten years ago. Our interests kept converging. Then he offered me the spot at Sunquest about eight years ago and I took it. I was at UCLA Medical Center then. Ever since we've been haranguing people to open up their checkbooks, making Sunquest even better. Jason's good at fund-raising, but it's not his favorite. I'm miserable at it, so I generally keep my focus on what we can achieve if we have better funding. It's a constant battle, though. And critical if we're to keep our fees sliding. If a patient has insurance, great. If they don't, we foot the costs ourselves. Nobody'll lose their life savings at Sunquest to save the life of someone they love. But we can't save the world, so we select our patients pretty carefully."

"Then Maisy doesn't have to worry about the money."

"It's taken care of."

"What did your grandfather think when you joined Sunquest?"

"Mac? He bragged to all his cronies. Made noises about moving out here to Arizona. Retirement capital of the western U.S. But he never did. He was too tied to the ranch."

"And your mother? Did you see much of her after she left you with your grandfather?" She caught his hand as it ventured over the curve of her breast, and dragged it down to safer zones.

"She sent cards at Christmas for a while, then even that petered out. Mac tried to locate her when Bethany died, but he never found her. I tried too, the year I graduated from med school. No luck."

"What would you have done if you'd been successful?"

He found himself missing her button-down dresses. The one she wore now was like a shield of denim across her front, no hope of sneaking in a fingertip. "I don't know," he said. "Made sure she was okay, I guess."

"But why? She abandoned you and your sister."

"She made sure we were somewhere safe, first," Luke said. "I told you. We were better off with Mac. But," he sighed, "she was my mother."

Mel didn't say anything after that. He almost thought she might have fallen asleep, she was so still against him. When she did speak, it wasn't another question.

"I want to see you accept that award, Luke. People want to thank you, and you never let them. I want to go to the benefit."

"Mel, you don't have to prove anything to me."

"I have something to prove to myself," she said quietly.

And what could he say to that? "Okay."

They stayed on that chaise all night. Finally dropping off to sleep only to awaken with the warmth of the sun shining over them. Luke rose and took Mel by the hand and led her inside, where he slowly pulled her denim dress over her head. When she lifted her hands, reaching for his shirt, he caught them, kissed her knuckles. "Let me."

"But your bandage, your hand—"

"Let me."

Her lips parted. She slowly straightened her fingers, then relaxed them, curling them softly, trustingly over his. "All right." Her voice was barely a whisper.

He kissed her knuckles again. Released her only long enough to tear off his shirt, then turned her palms upward and kissed the vulnerable pulse throbbing on her smooth inner wrists. She made a soft sound, that little hum, and he clamped down on his sudden urge to rush. To devour.

Her fingers flexed again, brushing against his face. His throat. He tasted the inside of her elbow. She murmured his name. He tucked his fingers under the straps of her bra and steadily drew them down her shoulders. Her breasts, full, velvety, rose above the soft, white cups, filling his hands. The early sun shone through the windows, golden and warm on her flesh, his hands. She felt soft yet strong, but it was her eyes that held him captive. They looked heavy, dark, full of want.

He dragged his thumbs around, over her tight nipples. Her eyelashes dipped. He repeated the motion, and she pressed her lips softly together. Her throat worked as she swallowed. His jaw felt locked with need and he deliberately unclasped her bra, letting it fall where it may. Her white slip felt slippery under his fingers as he knelt and pulled it down, taking her panties along with it.

He straightened and slid his palm over the thrust of her belly that nestled against him. She sucked in her breath, audibly. Her hands covered his. She was trembling.

He was a doctor. There were no secrets the body possessed that he hadn't studied or examined. But the feeling running through him now had only one name. Wonder.

A single, glistening tear stood out on her lashes.

Patience gone, Luke lifted her in his arms and carried her to his bed. Her arms lifted toward him and as he went down beside her, he thought maybe, just maybe, he must have done something right along the way to deserve her, after all.

Lydia Frame picked up Mel on the dot of ten o'clock, and they drove into old town Scottsdale where little shops and boutiques lined the narrow streets. ''We have more malls than Carter's has pills,'' Lydia said, ''but I think the most interesting things can be found down here.''

''Well,'' Mel said as she stood on the sidewalk and felt heat radiate back at her from the cement, ''as long as the shops are cool. I always thought stories of the Arizona heat had to be exaggerated. But it's like the inside of an overheated Laundromat dryer, here.''

Lydia laughed and led her into the first of many perfectly lovely, perfectly cooled shops. By noon, Mel had found a dress. Lydia's running commentary on everything from her grandchildren to Sunquest's funding challenges to how much she enjoyed her visits to Turnabout ceased only when they stopped for a quick lunch. But it started up again as soon as they were inside

Lydia's long Lincoln with the air-conditioning blasting over them.

"It'll be good to have this benefit tonight out of our hair," she said. "Then I can concentrate on my next project."

"You do a lot for Dr. Frame's career, I suppose."

"Well, I support Jason, of course." She drove through the busy weekend traffic with ease. "When I can. It was just handy that I could help with the benefit. Ordinarily I'm busy enough with my own dog and pony shows for the school where I teach. It's appalling how badly budgets have been cut lately. To the point we have to raise our own money to support the music and arts programs. Disgraceful."

Mel stared at Lydia. "I didn't know you were a teacher."

"Oh, heavens, yes. Twenty-five years now. I hope to retire next year." She grinned. "More time for golf and grandbabies. Not necessarily in that order."

"You never mentioned it."

"Well, darling, it's not as if you and I ever really had a chance to sit down and chat much when Jason and I visited Turnabout. You were always the soul of discretion and hospitality, going about your job there. And while I'm proud of my career, I have to say I tend to brag far more about my grandchildren when given an opportunity. We'll have great fun, Mel. Assuming you do stay here with Luke, of course, I mean." She flushed a little. "There's a group of women, most of them wives from Sunquest in fact, and we get together once a week for breakfast."

"And plan fund-raisers," Mel presumed weakly.

"Good God, no." The notion seemed to truly horrify Lydia. "We kibitz and laugh and complain and do whatever suits our fancy. Some of us are grandmothers, some, like you are just starting out with their families. We all know it's not always easy being involved with a man with a calling, whether it's as a doctor or a minister or what have you. But it's not as if their life is our only life. Now, do you want me to drop you off at Sunquest, since I know that's where Luke is, or do you want me to drop you at his place?"

"Sunquest," Mel said faintly.

Lydia just smiled brilliantly and headed up the driveway to the clinic. "Do you like golf, Mel?"

"Never tried it."

"Ha." She parked in front of the main door. "Fresh blood." She laughed and waved as she drove off, leaving Mel standing there holding her shopping bags and a wealth of unsettlingly new perspective. It took only a moment for the baking heat to drive her inside, and she dumped her purchases in Luke's office then headed down to visit with Maisy and April. After a few hours with them, she went back to Luke's office. She knew he was doing consultations most of the day, but he'd expected to be through early enough so they could get ready for that evening.

He wasn't there, yet, though.

Before she could think better of it, she sat down at his desk and picked up the phone, dialing quickly. It was answered on the second ring, as it had always been.

"Hello, Reeves," she greeted. She nervously wound

the coiled phone cord around her finger. "It's Melanie.
I'd like to speak to Mother."

"Have I told you that you're beautiful?"

Mel smiled and tilted her head back to look at Luke.
The benefit had been underway for two hours. Luke
had received his award, they'd shaken dozens of hands,
posed for dozens of photos, met dozens of people. Now
they were dancing and Luke had made it plain that as
far as he was concerned, their time was officially their
own.

"I believe you might have mentioned it," Mel said.
She felt beautiful. Her soft brown dress bared her
shoulders, a good portion of her back, and a hint of
cleavage, didn't exaggerate just how pregnant she was,
and ended at the floor, hiding ankles that, for once,
weren't even puffy. But the most glorious part of it
was dancing with Luke. He'd shaved. He'd even gone
so far as to cut his hair. And as much as she had fancied
his mane of wild waves, she personally found his close-
cropped do particularly mouthwatering. Maybe because
it didn't distract from his thoroughly masculine features. "You look swell, yourself," she said. In a con-
servative tux that made her fingers itch to delve beneath.

His lips tilted, as if he'd divined her thoughts. "You
dance pretty well for a pregnant lady."

"I can do other things pretty well, also."

His eyes darkened. "Ms. Summerville, are you
threatening me with—what did you call it—bed bouncing?"

She slid her arm around his neck and lifted her

mouth close to his ear. "Promising. But first, I have something I want to give you. I was saving it for the right moment."

Luke's eyes drifted downward. "There's nothing else you can give me that matters more than this."

"All right, so it's a gift for Sunquest." She slid out of his arms and headed back to the table they'd shared with the Frames and some members of the governor's staff. Her heart pounded, not just from Luke's proximity, but because she wasn't entirely certain how he would react to what she'd done. She lifted her little crocheted purse that went with the dress and plucked the check from inside. "Here," she blurted, handing it to him. "I don't want you to think that I'm doing this for any reason other than that I believe in what Sunquest does."

He looked from her to the check. "What are you talking about?"

"It's a donation." She nibbled her lip. "I, um, I talked to my parents today, Luke. And told them that I finally had a use for the trust fund I've tried to ignore most of my life. My father had the funds wired this afternoon. Figures that he'd be able to get around little details like banks being closed on Saturday afternoons."

He didn't even glance at the writing. "You talked to them? When? Why?"

"Because of you." She realized that it might have been better to wait until they were home before announcing things this way. They were in the grand ballroom of the famed Arizona Biltmore, surrounded by hundreds of guests, though mostly nobody was paying them any heed at the moment. "Because you tried to find your mother, despite all that happened. Because you're decent and kind and you don't deserve a wife who's afraid to face up to the disappointments of her past."

"Wife?"

She swallowed. "Luke, the check is a gift, no matter what. No strings, no expectations. It's just that I can finally put the money somewhere that I believe in."

"Wife?"

"No matter what happens Monday morning, with April, I know you'll do your best for her. Whether or not that means you'll scrub, or oversee or what—"

Luke covered her mouth with his bandaged hand and watched her eyes go wide. *"Wife?"*

She blinked. Nodded jerkily. Carefully lifted his hand away from her mouth. "And I think we should probably do it soon, 'cause you know twins sometimes have a tendency to come early. And my parents will probably want to come, too, so it's only right to give you fair warning. As long as it's before fall session begins at the university. He's the dean, you see, and—"

"Mel."

"—what?"

"Shut up."

Her mouth snapped closed.

"I'm going to say this once and you listen well. I'm glad you called your parents. For your sake. But you never, *ever*, have to do something because you think I expect it. I don't give a flying flip who or what your parents are, except that they did something right in creating you. I love you. I want a life with you. With our children. I want a partner, not a pretty prop. I want— what are you crying for?''

She dashed away a tear. ''You haven't said that before.''

''Said what?''

''That you love me.''

He gave her a long look. ''What do you think the past month has been about, Mel? I love you. I've loved you from the night you seduced me on the beach.''

''I didn't—''

''You did. We did. And it's been my sanity when there wasn't anything sane left about me. The sooner you're my wife, the happier I'll be.''

''It's not just about the babies?''

''It's never been just about the babies,'' he said, his voice raw. If he started kissing her, he wasn't going to stop. Which meant he needed to get her alone. ''I suppose you're gonna want a wedding, all the trimmings and fuss.''

''I've done all that, Luke. And none of it matters. What matters is the man who shares the vows. I don't care if we have a hundred guests or a mere handful. As long as my parents and Maisy and April are there, and Jason and Lydia, too, I think, we'll have everyone who truly matters.''

''And if April—''

''Shh. I don't even want to hear it. I have faith in you, Luke. In you. In us. In the incredible fact that we ever met at all that night. And I have faith that April will come through this, healthier and better than ever before because of you and everyone else at Sunquest.''

"Mel, my hand is able, but that doesn't necessarily mean I'll be—"

"You will." Her lips softened, pressed against his. "Have faith, Luke. You're the one who told me that. Trust your heart. Have faith. We have one more chance. The rest will come."

He cupped her face in his palm and ran his thumb down the fine line of her jaw. Stared into the depths of her mesmerizing eyes and saw the truth there. The truth and the peace that had bound him to her from the very start. "You really believe that."

Her cheek pressed into his hand, her eyes never straying from his. "I believe in you, Luke. I believe in us," she said.

And that was all they needed.

Epilogue

Mel hugged her arms against her body and stared out the window to the desert landscape beyond. It seemed as if days had passed since Luke had disappeared behind the double doors of O.R. 2. In truth, it had only been a few hours.

But with each minute that ticked by, the atmosphere in the small waiting area seemed to grow ever more silent. More tense. Mel looked over at Maisy, who sat still as a statue, on the upholstered couch. She hadn't moved once since Luke went in to scrub.

"She's going to make it," Mel said quietly.

Maisy swallowed and nodded. Even her red curls looked subdued today. "I'll never forget the day Tessa told me she was pregnant." Her hands lifted then fell back to her lap, twisting together. "I was…horrified. She hadn't been seeing anyone that I knew of. She never once told me who he was. April's father. But she loved him, I never doubted that. I could see it in her face. Then April came along.'' Her throat worked. ''Losing Tessa was bad enough,'' she said unsteadily. ''April has to come through.''

Mel sat down beside Maisy and closed her hand over the other woman's. If she was nervous, she knew Maisy's nerves were stretched far more thinly. ''Luke told us the surgery would take—'' She broke off at the hushed whoosh of the double doors opening.

Maisy sat forward in her seat, her grip on Mel's hand tight.

Jason Frame stepped into view. He looked tired, but as his gaze fell on the women, a small smile stretched his lips. ''She's being moved to recovery,'' he said without preamble. ''If you want to come with me, Maisy, you can sit with her for a few minutes. Luke will be out soon.''

Maisy nodded, her eyes red-rimmed. She squeezed Mel's hand and rose, looking shaky on her cumbersome cast. Jason tucked his hand under her arm and gently helped her through the double doors.

Mel pressed her hand to her heart and sank back against the couch. She closed her eyes, thanks coursing through her mind. Then she heard that whoosh again, and she opened her eyes to see Luke.

Luke, wearing pale green scrubs with a white hand towel slung around his neck, his hair sticking up in damp spikes. She pushed to her feet. ''You look like you've just gone ten rounds.''

''With a seven-year-old prizefighter,'' he said, his lips tilting. ''You, on the other hand, look beautiful.'' He stepped close and hooked his hands over her shoulders, pulling her against him. He lowered his head, resting it on her shoulders, and let out a long breath.

Mel wrapped her arms around him, loving him so much it felt as if she'd always loved him. "Are you okay?"

"Should be asking that about April."

Mel tilted her head against his, pressing her lips against his temple. She slid her fingers through his sweat-damp hair. "I know April is okay."

Luke breathed in the sweet, clean scent of her. He'd spend a lifetime earning the faith she had in him. He lifted his head until he could see into her eyes. And he felt the jolt he always did when she looked at him, inside him, and soul recognized soul. "She's got weeks of recovery ahead of her. We won't know conclusively until—"

"Shh." She pressed her lips against his. "How are *you* doing?"

His hand hurt like hell. And it was true that he felt as if he'd just fought his way out of a boxing ring. "Never better. Do you want to go back and see April? I have an in with the nurses back there."

"I'll bet you do," said Mel wryly. "Half the nurses here want to marry you and the other half want to adopt you."

"What do you want?"

"To marry you. To have our babies. Maybe more."

He raised his eyebrows. "More?"

"Well, it's fun to try," Mel pointed out sedately.

Only the fact that they were in the waiting room where any member of the staff could find them kept him from kissing her the way he wanted. "How about you? Are you okay?"

"Why wouldn't I be? I have everything I ever wanted in the palm of my hands."

"Your concern for April goes deeper than simple friendship," Luke said quietly. It was inextricably linked with memories of her son.

Mel studied him for a moment. How had it happened that he knew her so well? Or that she could read his thoughts, his emotions, as easily, maybe better, than her own?

"Dominic will always be with me, a beautiful little boy," she said. "If it weren't for him, for the short life he had, I wouldn't have met Maisy and found Turnabout. Or you. It's all a path. Our lives. The people we've known, and loved, let go and found." She slid her palms against his, linking their hands. "Now I'm on the path with you. And our family. I have more happiness than I'd ever thought I could find and I know that no matter what turns our path might have, we'll walk them together."

"Turnabout is quite a place," he said.

"A little sand, a little surf and a little magic." She leaned against him and he could feel the uneven movements of the babies inside her. "But the magic we keep with us wherever we go."

He decided he didn't give a flip if a staff member strolled in and found him kissing his fiancée. "I love you, Melanie Summerville."

Her lips curved against his. "I love you, too, Dr. Trahern."

* * * * * *

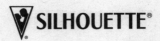

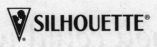
♥ SILHOUETTE®

1006/23b

SPECIAL EDITION™

TAMING A DARK HORSE
by Stella Bagwell
Men of the West

After suffering serious burns, loner Linc Ketchum
needed Nevada Ortiz's help. The sassy home nurse
brought Linc back to health and kindled a flame in his
heart. Now Nevada needed to find a cure…for Linc's
wounded spirit.

HEARD IT THROUGH THE GRAPEVINE
by Teresa Hill

A preacher's daughter was not supposed to be pregnant
and alone. But that's exactly what Cathie Baldwin was…
until Matthew Monroe, the local bad boy, came along
and offered the protection of his name and wealth.

HER SPECIAL CHARM by Marie Ferrarella
The Cameo

Detective James Munro knew the cameo he'd found
was no ordinary trinket. But little did he know what his
find would lead to—for the cameo's owner, beautiful
Southern belle Constance Beaulieu, seemed to want to
claim him, too.

Don't miss out!
On sale from 20th October 2006

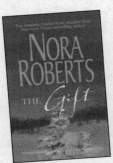

4 FREE

BOOKS AND A SURPRISE GIFT!

We would like to take this opportunity to thank you for reading this Silhouette® book by offering you the chance to take FOUR more specially selected titles from the Special Edition™ series absolutely FREE! We're also making this offer to introduce you to the benefits of the Mills & Boon® Reader Service™—

★ **FREE home delivery**
★ **FREE gifts and competitions**
★ **FREE monthly Newsletter**
★ **Exclusive Reader Service offers**
★ **Books available before they're in the shops**

Accepting these FREE books and gift places you under no obligation to buy, you may cancel at any time, even after receiving your free shipment. Simply complete your details below and return the entire page to the address below. You don't even need a stamp!

YES! Please send me 4 free Special Edition books and a surprise gift. I understand that unless you hear from me, I will receive 6 superb new titles every month for just £3.10 each, postage and packing free. I am under no obligation to purchase any books and may cancel my subscription at any time. The free books and gift will be mine to keep in any case.

E6ZED

Ms/Mrs/Miss/Mr .... Initials ....
BLOCK CAPITALS PLEASE

Surname ....

Address ....

....

.... Postcode ....

Send this whole page to:
UK: FREEPOST CN81, Croydon, CR9 3WZ